I0544842

The Blessing of Queen

Esjay C. Moore

The Blessing of Queen

Copyright 2017 Esjay C. Moore
Published by Sandmour Publishing

First edition 2017
All rights reserved. No part of this book may be
reproduced or transmitted in any form or by any means,
electronic or mechanical, including photocopying,
recording or any information storage or retrieval system
without permission from the copyright holder.
This story is a work of fiction. Names, characters,
businesses, organisations, places, events and incidents
are the product of the author's imagination or are used
fictitiously. Any resemblance to actual persons, living or
dead, events, or locales is entirely coincidental.
Any branded items referred to within the storyline
remain the full property of the relevant trademark or
copyright holder.

ISBN 978-0-620-77716-2 (print)
eISBN 978-0-620-77717-9 (e-book)

Cover Design & Interior Formatting: StarLoveNova
Cover Photo: Lvnel/Bigstock.com
Image used under license from bigstock.com

To all of you wonderful, beautiful women,
never let anyone hold you down.
Keep on rising like the queens that you are!
Believe in yourself and chase those dreams

To my invincible mother, Gwenythe
You continue to inspire me.
Thank you!

Blessing (noun) *a special favour, mercy, or benefit.*

In South Africa, an act of 'blessing' involves a 'blesser' (usually a wealthy married man) bestowing extravagant gifts and a luxury lifestyle upon a 'blessee' (usually a young and attractive female) in exchange for her company.

Mopantokobogo (proper noun) *origin: Zulu, meaning: "big man"*

Contents

CHAPTER ONE

The sexy sounds of soft jazz oozed sensuously through the luxury top-floor Rosebank apartment. Dappled shadows danced seductively against the expansive windows, while the living room walls basked lazily in the warm embrace of the setting sun. The sleek marble floors and original artworks spoke of someone with infinite style and sophistication. Perhaps an investment banker or an international hotelier, but most definitely someone with financial reach.

In the boudoir sits a half-naked woman attending to her appearance in front of a large, gilded mirror. Her freshly moisturised coffee-toned skin is smooth and supple, and hints to the vibrancy of her youth.

It was not always this way, Queen thought to herself as she guided her 'true-black' eyeliner to a perfect elongated flick.

OK let' us pause for a moment!

I might as well tell you now, that "Queen" is not her real name. In fact, so different was her start in life that it could not be any less royal if she had tried. Queen was born in the foothills of KwaZulu-Natal as Mbali.

Mbali Mthethwa, the fourth daughter born to a single mother, living in the single room of a mud hut. She was by no means a queen, but just another unplanned mouth to feed.

Despite this predicament, her mother Nandi loved her babies, but through bad choices found herself repeating the cycle of hoping the next man she lay with, would fulfil his promise to take care of them. Alas, those promises were just the cunning utterances to achieve only one dishonourable intention. As soon as the opportunist discovered that Nandi was with child, the empty promises that she once clasped so close to her heart, slipped like water through her fingers.

By the time Mbali was a bubbly and bright six-year-old, a baby brother Mandla had joined the brood. Of course, the intended saviour to the growing family had long since departed in a trail of dust. The mere existence of this young female-headed family living in the rural countryside was a desperate routine of living hand-to-mouth. Wondering where the next paltry meal would come.

Nandi made the heart-wrenching decision to leave her babies behind, to pursue opportunities for better wages in the nearest town of Pietermaritzburg. And so, little Mbali and her siblings found themselves in the care of their loving grandmother, Gogo Isisa. As much love as Gogo gave, she offered little knowledge regarding life experiences outside of the dusty kraal village. When school began for Miss Mbali Mthethwa, it was indeed a wondrous affair, even if it meant she must leave before sun-up to walk many miles, to the humble farm school.

Like her namesake, Mbali was as lovely and as fragile as the wildflowers that dotted the summery landscape, but what shone most was her yearning to discover all the majestic wonders of life. Mbali's eyes sparkled when she learnt of people who shaped the world for future generations, improving the lives of others through meaningful technological advancements, or sheer generosity and kindness.

The pictures and stories and even the songs were all a welcomed treat, but most welcomed was the warm, starchy meal offered to fill her belly. The simple black school dress was much too big for her petite frame, and it scratched her delicate skin. But, to Mbali, this was a small sacrifice to endure for her love affair with life, school, and everything in between.

It was not much longer than two months after Mama Nandi had left, before the first box arrived addressed to Gogo Isisa. The box contained a letter, neatly folded around a R200 note, telling of Nandi's employment with the "van Rensburg family" in Hatfield. She painted a picture of a decent family with two mischievous boys, whom she must care for while both parents were at work. In exchange, she received a small room, basic food supplies and a weekly wage. Also in the box, were modest, yet colourful trinkets for each of her young offspring, designed more to distract from the fact that their Mama was not with them.

Every three months or so, these simple cardboard 'treasure chests', along with what little cash Nandi could spare, arrived at the mud hut as a gentle reminder of her love and longing. As intended, the boxes brought much giddy excitement and laughter, as each compared their gifts of 'Made in China' t-shirts, fluffy toys and costume jewellery.

A lifestyle as modest as those memories, certainly was not the case for Queen now. In stark contrast, her wardrobes bulged with copious amounts of designer labels, and drawers filled with expensive jewellery fit for royalty.

The iPod changed tracks seamlessly as Queen stood to make her way to this evening's chosen ensemble hanging from the door of her closet. The exquisite full-length gown of shimmering silk was carefully selected by her suitor this summer's evening. The tastefully provocative design was guaranteed to elicit the attention of onlookers. She carefully slipped the silky sapphire-coloured evening dress off its hanger. Stepping into the free-flowing fabric, Queen adjusted the straps over her smooth shoulders. The rich, vibrant blue perfectly complemented her glowing complexion, and the

4

expertly seamed fabric fell effortlessly as it skimmed over her endless curves. Manoeuvring her svelte frame before zipping the side, Queen admired her elegance in the full-length mirror. She would never have believed that such wealth would surround her at just 22.

Mbali had excelled at school. As the years passed, she proved to be nothing short of a sponge; hungry for knowledge. She hoped that one day she could be the first in her family to get her matriculation certificate. The first to go to university to qualify as a teacher, so she could one day encourage other hungry young minds to also reach for the stars. Just like her favourite teacher Miss Sithole.

For now, Queen reached for her expensive French perfume, before slipping her feet into a pair of gem-encrusted *Louboutins*.

There was a perfectly timed knock at the door.

A solid masculine knock.

CHAPTER TWO

Opening the door with an ingratiating smile, Queen greeted a distinguished gentleman in an expensive suit. At first glance, he may have easily passed for her father, but it was the familiar greeting that hinted at a far more intimate relationship.

Queen seductively secured the last of her sparkly chandelier earrings to her ear. "You're right on time as usual," Queen said leaning into Kgabu's muscular chest to kiss him on the cheek. His one hand firmly planted in the hollow of her bare back.

"If I had known you were going to look this radiantly appetising, I would've arrived earlier," he jested, allowing his hand to wander down over her 'juicy curves', as he liked to call them.

Kgabu Mokae - an influential businessman at the top of his game in a city that never sleeps. A captain of industry and an esteemed money mogul. He began his empire, a computer repairs shop, from a borrowed garage with modest funds, but worked tirelessly to build his IT business from the ground up. It required the same fervent determination which he still practices in his current business dealings.

Now, 40-years later, Kgabu owns not just an international IT company with lucrative government contracts, but a string of other successful businesses ranging from import-export, communication networks reaching up into Africa, a national media house and a substantial stake in a truly African-owned private bank. Such success has yielded significant financial benefits, which was a good thing, for as long as his wife was taken care of financially, she chose to ignore his wandering eye and penchant for beautiful ladies.

For a 59-year-old, Kgabu appears younger than his years. His broad 6-foot frame hints at a man who takes good care of himself; his lightly salted goatee contrasting his dark complexion and outlines his wonderfully wicked smile. It is evident before he even speaks a word, why Kgabu is such a hit with the ladies.

Apart from his wife and Queen, there was a string of other beautiful young nymphs longing to be at his beck and call. Kgabu was not faithful, never had been, and probably never would be, but he was generous and kind. He knew the rewards of treating each lady as if she was the only one that matters.

Queen settled herself into the plush white leather of the Bentley. Kgabu slid in beside her as his driver ushered the door closed, behind them. His eyes looked longingly at his beautiful young Queen seated comfortably next to him. His steady hand brushed the liquid blue silk from her knee, revealing what he believed were her best assets.

"Legs for miles," he murmured, lightly tracing the curved lines of her smooth legs with the back of his fingertips.

As much as he yearned for her, their trysts did not involve sex. Instead, their unique relationship reflected the meeting of two brilliant minds, celebrated through the sheer indulgence of an intimate appreciation of each other's beautiful form. For Kgabu touch had always been titillating, besides at his age gratification was more than just rampant sex, but often brought from a pleasurable tête-à-tête, involving sensual massages tangled up in crispy cotton sheets. He trusted that Queen would know when and if the time would be right, and while his desire for her was rising, he merely enjoyed the sweetness of the journey for now.

He leaned in to kiss her neck breathing in her essence as he did. "The scent of your bare skin … it's magical," he whispered.

Queen lightly brushed the side of his face with her hand, "I should hope that you like it Kgabu, my Warrior." She smiled alluringly, "it is the fragrance you brought me from your travels last week."

Queen understood how men just loved to be reminded of the gifts they bestowed upon their ladies. She also knew that such appreciative reminders coupled with a devoted look or lingering touch, especially in front of other would-be challengers, would ensure future gifts of even greater magnitude. After all, this had become her business over the last six years.

Her lean legs, freshly moisturised, glimmered in the passing streetlights as the Bentley moved swiftly towards the convention centre. Tonight, Kgabu was sponsoring the 'Young Entrepreneur of the Year Awards', as he had done for the last three years.

Queen would stand flawlessly by Kgabu's side this evening. Some observers might ignorantly assume she was one of his protégées, but others would jealously consider her as being a mere trophy, further representing the pinnacle of success he had achieved. For him, she was a friend, a confidant, and a sweet escape from his everyday stresses.

The gala dinner attracted close to 1,000 patrons, and at R3,000.00 a ticket it was a stylish affair; drawing those with more money than the time in which to spend it. None-the-less the event was a great networking opportunity for ambitious business leaders.

Seated at Table One of 100, Queen was the youngest at the event, apart from a handful of ambitious nominees. As expected, her youthful appearance did not go unnoticed by the female guests, who held their suspicions behind clenched teeth and fake smiles as they tried to impress Kgabu. Their husbands held an entirely different opinion of the situation, secretly envious of Kgabu's fortunate predicament.

Queen took her seat quietly sipping champagne, while Kgabu made his expected rounds of slapping rotund tuxedo-clad men on the back; discussing the 'good old days' at the prestigious college he had attended, or this and that sports happening at 'Uni'. It was all a little too much for Queen, for it was a sad reminder of a chapter in her life that she always dreamt of, but never had the opportunity to actualise.

"Gooooooood evening everyone!" an unfamiliar jovial voice sounded next to Queen. She turned and saw a pleasant-looking man in his early forties, with an unruly mop of sandy brown hair and happy blue eyes, take the seat next to her.

"Good evening," she said, holding out her hand to shake his, "I'm Queen."

"Well, I'm impressed!" He said. "For once the booking agent fulfilled my request to be seated next to the prettiest lady in the house." He gave her a cheeky wink, "Please no need to frisk me, I do have a legitimate ticket to be here despite my appearance! Oh, and before I dig my hole any deeper, I'm Mathew Tillman." He began to show signs of blush, as he squirmed in his chair.

"I think your crater just got deeper Mathew!" Queen could not contain her smile as she teased him innocently.

Mathew was a breath of fresh air in an otherwise stale room, but it had not gone unnoticed that he arrived single, and no wedding band to show. *Surely now the judgemental ladies can relax in knowing their husbands are safe. As if they were ever in jeopardy!* Queen thought somewhat smugly.

The completely natural conversation between Queen and Mathew was well underway when Kgabu glanced across the room. Although engaged in a more serious discussion of his own, it was not long before he manoeuvred his way back to the table.

"Mathew, my friend!" Kgabu announced extending his broad hand to the handsome newcomer.

Mathew stood to shake Kgabu's hand, "Mannnn we have to stop meeting like this!"

Kgabu took his seat on the other side of Queen to continue his conversation with Mathew. As it turns out, Mathew ran Kgabu's operations at the media giant. They intended to cement their presence into Africa, through the establishment of localised news agencies catering to those specific markets. The once exuberant conversation had suddenly become all too 'blah-blah-serious' for

Queen, as she quietly resorted to her tall crystal flute of French bubbly.

After 20 minutes or so, Kgabu adjusted his gold cufflinks and stood up.

"Well, if you could both excuse me, I need to prepare to make my grand speech now. Trust you will enjoy it." As he spoke, he allowed his warm hand to linger a little on Queen's bare shoulder as a gentle reminder of his craving for her.

Listening to Kgabu speak so effortlessly with charm and wisdom, it was no wonder he was so greatly respected. The crowd remained riveted to their seats basking in his profound words of encouragement, exceptional achievements to date and his staunch belief in the upcoming entrepreneurial stars. Queen could not help but think back to her previous life when Mbali would have also awakened the spirit of achievement in others.

She took another sip.

Between dinner courses, Kgabu flitted back and forth from the dinner table to engage with other familiar faces in the room. His fleeting attendance did not perturb Queen as she was enjoying the continued enthusiasm of Mathew's captivating conversation. She wondered if perhaps it was that he was close to twenty years younger than the other men in her life, or that he did not show the seriousness or pretence that they did. There was some form of chemistry; perhaps even some destiny that brought them together, but for now, it was merely a frivolous distraction.

Then out of the blue Mathew looked serious for a moment. "Queen? Do you think I could be cheeky enough to ask for your number?"

Such a question was not entirely foreign to Queen, and yet she was astonished, considering that she was here with Kgabu, and Mathew was not just his guest, but his friend. She paused, perhaps a little too long as she considered the request.

"I'm sorry I asked! Hell Queen, you can't blame a guy for trying!" Assuming he might have offended her, Mathew attempted backpedalling.

She bit her lip momentarily, wondering whether this was truly a request as a friend or an appeal to enter her 'elite circle'. The fact that he was single and not needing the usual discreetness, surely hinted at the former and she finally responded with her usual exuberance.

"Absolutely Mathew! Perhaps we could do coffee during the week?"

"Champion!" He said.

Champion? She thought, *what is this? Sports simulcast?* It was then that Queen realised Mathew was just a clumsy man holding little finesse with the ladies.

From the other side of the room, Kgabu did not miss Mathew passing his little white business card but considering his own fidelity issues, he was not one to get jealous or possessive. He understood the cogwheels of this relationship and respected the fact that many wished to be honoured by Queen's presence. Besides, he knew this was a brief tryst in her life and soon she would find something far more meaningful and fulfilling than being a mere trophy for a wealthy old man.

Kgabu still questioned himself as he watched the two of them, *why am I so threatened when this is the same scenario in which I met her?* Not paying attention to the discussion at hand, his mind wandered to the evening in question. At first, he had not noticed Queen at the charity event, but when she raised her bidding paddle #16 in opposition to his, he was entirely captured by the presence of her in that graceful red ballgown.

The feisty 'bidding war' began over an abstract masterpiece and although the battle lasted no more than a few minutes, it set the stage for the subsequent game of cat and mouse. Kgabu and Queen dodged their significant others to eventually find a fleeting moment to enjoy a flirtatious introduction. There was mutual attraction, or so he believed, yet something even deeper than that, which he could not explain. It was not the cliché 'love at first sight' or even lust, but something more palpable like an immense respect for the essence of this striking young woman.

That evening Queen's company was none other than the dubious politician Isaac Mopantokobogo. Kgabu's initial reaction was: *What is such an innocent beauty, doing with someone of such ill reputation?* His secondary instinct told him that this was a mutually beneficial arrangement, and yet this still troubled him.

Rumours of how Isaac manipulated his position in public office to benefit his personal agenda had gained momentum in recent years. Yet no matter the charges brought against Isaac, he always managed to slip through the courts unblemished.

Kgabu knew this man could not be trusted.

CHAPTER THREE

Two years after Mama had left her babies in the care of Gogo Isisa, a suspicious-looking letter arrived. It was Gogo who explained the gravity of contents to the children.

"My little ones, the family for whom Mama has worked, for almost two years is leaving the country. So, she finds that she is out of work now," Gogo tried to disguise her trembling voice with a discreet cough.

She continued, knowing that what was to follow could not be good news. "Mama has heard of a man, a Mr Mthunzi, who is offering jobs in Durban, so she is going to see him. As soon as she settles, she will write, but she writes that you are all forever in her heart." Gogo looked up from the letter to see a row of wide eyes looking at her, all-knowing that yet again the family would be entering a time of even less money. As it was, the meagre pittance of the social grant could barely cover the staples they needed, so the uplifting parcels from Nandi had always been a great help.

Sadly, that was the last letter the family ever received from Nandi. Gogo sent desperate inquiries through the 'friendship grapevine' to inquire about her daughter and this Mr Mthunzi, but all returned without news.

As the years passed, the two older sisters left school prematurely, and shortly afterwards they left the dusty village to work as cleaners at a nearby country retreat. The four girls had not seen much of each other since, but always believed that one day they would once again be together with their mother, their brother and Gogo.

Mbali was now 16 and still making her teachers proud. Her older sister Ayize was not as bright as Mbali, but equally eager to learn. Although Ayize found it difficult to keep her grades up, it was still humiliating for her to hear that she could not progress with the rest of her class to her final year. As sad as Ayize was, for Mbali this was a most fortunate happening.

"Now we can sit next to each other in class, and help each other with homework!" Announced Mbali with her usual positive attitude. She went on further to remind Ayize about the story of the tortoise and the hare.

"It's not how quickly you get there Ayize!" She exclaimed, "it's that you get there exactly when you should!" Ayize hugged Mbali tightly, for she always knew the right thing to say, and so Ayize chose to make the most of the situation.

One sunny Saturday morning, Mbali and Ayize were attending to the laundry at the meandering stream. Their cheerful singing came to a halt when they noticed a pale blue car making its way up the rocky hillside road. They curiously watched as the car stopped with a loud clunk at their home. Ayize stood up, shading her eyes from the sun.

"Mbali! Mbali I think it's Mama!" Ayize dropped the clothes in a twisted pile and started stumbling up the stony hill barefooted. Mbali right behind her. The high-pitched sounds of a celebratory ululation rang in the air, causing unsuspecting neighbours to step outside their huts to see what the cause for such festivity was.

Alas the woman that now stood before them, although she held some resemblance to their beautiful mother, was frail and buckled over. Young Mandla and this strange man helped her to sit against the wall of their modest hut. The pain was overflowing in Mama's eyes, as tears streamed down her gaunt cheeks without even trying. The girls wiped the tears away, and stroked her hands gently, feeling the thin skin covering the brittle bones. Nandi shut her eyes and bravely attempted to smile, for the sake of her babies.

Gogo was in dialogue with this man, who was none other than the elusive Mr Mthunzi. He was waving a sheet of paper at Gogo, and repetitively pointing at Mama and then at the paper, his angry voice bellowing ever louder. Gogo was trembling and shaking her head as she fidgeted with her apron. There was something profoundly distressful about this discussion for the ageing matriarch. Noticing Gogo's anxiety, Mbali told Mandla to hold his mother's hand so that she could attend to Gogo.

Mr Mthunzi was a big man, who reeked of sour beer and cigarettes. He wore gold rings on every fat finger as if to display his wealth just like a peacock would display his feathers. Mbali would not be intimidated by his offensive appearance, or by his brash, bellowing voice.

"What is it you want with us?" She demanded.

He laughed at her. "You are a bold one aren't you!?" He retorted, "well if you must know I am Mr Mthunzi. I own a tavern in Durban, for which your mother has worked for many years." He folded the paper and placed it back into his pocket.

"...and so? What does that have to do with Gogo?" Mbali inquired matter-of-factly.

"I'm glad you asked Little Princess," he said condescendingly adjusting his pants under his overhanging belly. "Your mother has a contract with my establishment, and since she is unable to fulfil her obligation in her condition, and Gogo cannot afford to buy the contract, one of YOU little princesses will need to work in her place." He seemed quite impressed with himself, as he eyeballed Ayize's form.

19

"Let me see the paper!" Mbali insisted, pointing at his pocket.

Reaching into his pocket once more, Mr Mthunzi produced the tattered looking contract. "Here!" he said. "It is a copy of the original, so take it. Make a decision tonight, and tomorrow morning I will be back to collect one of you!" He turned to leave.

As he reached for the car door handle, he looked back at Mbali. "You better make a decision. If you fail to do so, I have friends that will come and take care of business, just the way they do in the cities." And with that Mr Mthunzi drove his pale blue clunking car back down the rocky hillside road.

Mbali fell quiet. Every bone in her body began to quiver. She knew nothing of contracts and obligations, but here was a stranger threatening to take her, or Ayize, away from their home. This implication did not seem fair, but there was the paper in her hands.

The girls gently bathed their weak mother in silence, noticing the bruises and sores littering her body. They placed her in an improvised, yet comfortable bed so that she could see the valley of her childhood through the open doorway. She was gravely ill, but how she reached this dire state they did not know. Together they sang the lullaby she would sing to them as babies, gently encouraging her to sip the hearty winter-soup Gogo had prepared earlier for supper. With their sweet angelic voices filling her broken heart, Mama drifted off to sleep.

Mbali and Ayize sat with Gogo by the crackling fire to discuss this dire situation. There was some talk of running away; calling the neighbours; or trying to raise the R12,000 this stranger demanded of them for the final two years of the contract. It was no use, they could not raise such monies, and if they resisted in any way, he would send men to 'take care of business'.

Finally, Ayize spoke. "I shall go! I am the oldest. Mbali can make something good of her life and for all the family."

Mbali hated to admit it, but Ayize's suggestion did make sense, but how could she be so selfish.

"No!" Mbali uttered forcefully. "Ayize you are too easily tricked. Let me go for I am stronger in mind."

And so, the conversation swayed to-and-fro all night, until through sheer exhaustion the sad little family fell asleep, huddled together around the flickering glow of a fading fire.

The next morning Mbali woke earlier than the others. She checked on her mother, who was still sleeping and went to sit on the rock at the top of the hill to watch the sunrise over the valley. She sat quietly for more than an hour; her young mind heavily burdened as she replayed the discussion with Mr Mthunzi from the day before. Then like the dawning sun, an epiphany came to her like a ray of light from the sky. She promptly rushed back down the hill to the hut to wake Ayize. Grabbing both hands in hers, Mbali looked at Ayize with wide eyes.

"We shall both go! Together we will offer Mr Mthunzi a year of each of our lives to make up the two years that is owed!" Mbali barely breathing from excitement. She gasped before continuing, "this way, we can take care of each other, and when the year is over, we can return to school and our family. It will be like just a short detour in our lives. Just one year!"

Ayize finally beamed, acknowledging the logic of the suggestion. She should have known Mbali would find the best solution for this perilous predicament. "Yes! This option could be worth suggesting to Mr Mthunzi!" Ayize almost squealed in agreement.

CHAPTER FOUR

The drive back to Queen's high-rise apartment was quiet. Kgabu appeared distracted. Finally, Queen broke the silence.

"Your speech was compelling tonight. You never cease to impress me with the generous manner you impart your wisdom with others."

"Thank you, Queen," he replied softly, placing his arm around her shoulders, and drawing her closer to his warmth.

"You seem a little tense," she said observing his preoccupation, "perhaps I could tempt you to enjoy the warmth of a lingering shower with me?"

Kgabu gave her arm a gentle squeeze, "I think I will not join you tonight, I am feeling a little tired from all the attention of this evening. I will just call it a night."

This response was a little out of character for Kgabu, as usually he was energised by having his business-ego stroked, but Queen was quite happy to just relax alone in her comfortable environs. Besides, the last few days her mind was drenched in thoughts of her lost youth. Perhaps she needed the last hours of this evening alone to reflect.

Maybe, the time was right for her to offer Kgabu something more than just the hands-on attention - at least before he got bored and moved on. Queen preferred to take it slow at the beginning of what she called: 'the arrangement'. Not only was this to encourage a better understanding of each other, but also to build up the anticipation. This helped her feel that the 'blessing' was more of a relationship, rather than prostituting herself. Besides, she felt more at ease knowing her partner's desires were at a peak, during the first moment of real intimacy. Unlike a few men before him, Kgabu understood Queen's motives and was prepared to wait for the perfect moment.

Queen leaned her head back against his shoulder and gave Kgabu a soft lingering kiss. She cared deeply for this man but always wondered what his wife failed to provide him. It had just started to rain and as she watched the trails of silver run down the window, she remembered the night she had met Kgabu. She believed it was kismet.

That evening of their meeting at the charity auction, Queen was being chauffeured back to her apartment. Next to her slouched a slurring, stinking, groping Isaac. She stared ahead as each wiper-blade erased the pelting rain from the windscreen. She had perfected the art of detachment, mostly at the hands of Isaac and it proved useful as a skill to her survival thus far. Tonight, Isaac would want his pound of flesh from her so that he could justify the expense of the luxury apartment and sporty convertible currently being afforded to her.

But tonight, she was fortunate to sit next to a true gent who would never dream to raise a hand. Queen's thoughts wandered, and soon she was smiling to herself recalling how Kgabu had initially asked for the 'honour' of her time. She had instinctively thought: *Well, he may have won the feisty 'bidding war', but I have won his attention, and let's just say I know that colourful masterpiece will hang sublimely in my entrance hall.*

True to her power of gentle persuasion, the abstract oil painting now hung in her apartment.

Colourful – Yes!

Sublimely – Yes!

But holding far less importance these days, as she re-evaluated her life's authenticity.

Breaking the silence and her moment of reminiscence, Kgabu spoke. "I am required to be in Cape Town on Tuesday!" He looked down to Queen's perfect face against his shoulder, "perhaps you could join me for an overnight trip? It's a business trip so you will need to keep yourself occupied during the day, but we could do some wining and dining in the evening. Just you and me."

Queen considered his suggestion for a moment wondering whether this would clash with the other, far less accommodating, man in her life. Unfortunately, Isaac came before all others.

"That would be marvellous! You know me I would shop for 24 hours if you let me!" She finally responded.

"Just as long as you make sure to purchase something enticing. Something that I would appreciate, then I am sure I will be a happy man." Kgabu murmured, not in a mean way but more in agreement.

This is how it was with Kgabu. He provided the financial means for her to do with as she liked. If it made her happy, he was happy. Queen always remained respectful that it was his money regardless of how easy it was for him to amass. It was an understood relationship of convenience from which they both benefited and held mutual regard.

CHAPTER FIVE

True to his word, the next day the now-familiar pale blue car came rumbling back up the hill.

Mr Mthunzi squeezed himself out from behind the wheel like a giant sardine escaping the tin and straightened his creased jacket before heading towards the hut.

A confident Mbali met him.

"So? What is it, Little Princess? Have you made a decision?" He muttered.

She pointed for him to sit on one of the makeshift stools, while she took the other. "Well Mr Mthunzi, we understand that you require one of us to work for two years at your tavern. As you know, Gogo is very old, and Mama is very sick ...."

He interrupted abruptly, "Yes, come on now I don't have all day to go through this again!" He removed a handkerchief to wipe the beads of perspiration from his clammy fat face.

"Fine. Then what I might suggest that instead of one of us going, that you consider taking both of us for just one year?" Mbali held her breath, hoping he would find this acceptable.

Mr Mthunzi rubbed his brow while pretending to consider the proposal when in fact he was thinking: *Acceptable? It is more than acceptable!*

This is a prize on a silver platter! These girls know nothing of what I will expect of them.

After a few minutes of pretence, Mr Mthunzi looked up from the ground, stretching out his pudgy arm to shake her slender hand. "Very well, Little Princess, we have a deal then!"

"One more thing Mr Mthunzi," she said assertively. "My name is not Little Princess, it is Mbali!"

Mr Mthunzi spoke to Gogo for a few minutes, telling her he would take care of the girls and assuring her that he would pay them well. He then gave her R500 for her 'trouble' which ironically, she thanked him for believing he was doing the struggling little family a momentous favour. In reality, it was 'guilt money'. Nothing but a bribe.

The young Mtwethwa girls knelt by Nandi to say goodbye, without wishing to alarm her to the situation.

"Mama, Ayize and I are going on a great adventure. Soon, we will be home to see you." Mbali whispered, "then we can sit together around the fire and describe all the exciting things we saw and did!" Holding back the tears, she continued, "we will laugh and laugh."

In turn, the young girls each kissed their mother's forehead, saying: "See you soon Mama." Brushing the grey dust from their knobbly knees, the naïve girls stood and left the hut.

After a few minutes of tearful goodbyes to Gogo and Mandla, the young duo picked up their small tattered brown suitcase together and walked to the car. It was a scary moment, not knowing where they were going, and what type of work they would do, but they promised Gogo to send word as soon as they could. Mr Mthunzi closed the door behind them with a loud thump.

The pale blue car soon hurtled down the dusty hillside for the last time. The girls peered from the back window, waving at Gogo and 10-year-old Mandla standing at the door of the disappearing hut.

CHAPTER SIX

The car hummed monotonously along the freeway heading south of Durban. The two girls watched the concrete buildings sliding past the window. They had not let each other's hand go since leaving home almost 30-minutes ago.

Not a word was spoken.

An aeroplane flew over the freeway swooping in lower until grey buildings hid it from sight. The girls watched with big eyes. To see a plane, not in a book, so close, was marvellous. Although the girls were 16 and 18, these naïve creatures had led a sheltered life tucked away in the rolling green hills. Right now, everything was bewildering as their senses filled.

The car continued past the airport before turning from the freeway. Over a bridge and soon the girls were being jerked and swayed as the car navigated the bumpy gravel road. The dusty streets were alive with people going about their Sunday morning rituals, each hollering good morning to the next with sweeping hand gestures and loud vocals.

At the intersection, the car took a hard left to enter a large newly tarred parking area, before eventually slowing to a complete halt. Mbali looked out the window towards the modern red brick building with a big red and white sign which read: "MTHUNZI'S TAVERN & VIP LOUNGE."

Mbali squeezed Ayize's hand and whispered anxiously, "My sister, we are here!"

Cautiously exiting the backseat, the girls looked at each other as Mr Mthunzi retrieved their modest suitcase from the boot of the car. He looked at the girls standing apprehensively next to the car door. "Well come on now, it's time to meet the others," he said gesturing towards the entrance.

The girls climbed the eight or so steps to the looming wooden-panelled door that was being held captive by the durable black painted metal gate. With a jingle of keys, Mr Mthunzi swung the creaky door open and nudged the girls through, making sure he slammed the gate closed behind them again. The girls looked around the large, foul-smelling room, bedecked with wooden floors and a ruby-red hue on the walls. There were endless black chairs stacked upon wooden slatted tables. Mr Mthunzi walked behind a long wooden bar and flipped the light switch, before taking two red soda cans from the glass fridge for each of the girls. The room flickered alive with bright neon lights bouncing iridescent colours from the mirrors. Unfortunately, this did not help dull the vinegary stench of spilt alcohol emanating from the floors, nor the sharpness of the bleach residue on the table surfaces. Mbali rubbed her irritated nose.

"Right! First things first!" Mr Mthunzi roared while passing them each a Cola, "from now on I am your father! So, you will call me Baba Mthunzi, or just Baba. Okay?"

The girls nodded.

"I can't hear you?" he responded, as he placed his sunglasses on top of his sweat-beaded head.

"Yes, Baba Mthunzi," they replied in unison.

"Right. Now come with me," he barked, making his way towards a black painted door.

The girls followed him through a maze of rooms, dark stairwells, and corridors. The muffled sound of laughter became increasingly louder. He knocked on a door, and a half-dressed man opened.

"Morning Boss!" The man said shifting his eyes from Baba Mthunzi to look the newcomers up and down.

"Hello Tau, listen these are the new girls. They are inexperienced, straight from the farm so you must take special care of them for me," Baba Mthunzi instructed sharply.

"Yes, Boss I will take special care of these gems for you," Tau replied with a creepy smirk.

Then looking at the girls, Baba Mthunzi announced, "This is Tau Maseko. He looks after the girls here if you have any problems with the other girls, or with the people that come here, you talk to Tau."

Once again, they nodded.

The laughter died down, leaving a scuffling sound mixed with bare footsteps running on a tiled floor. Mthunzi walked towards another gate. He unlocked it and shepherded the girls into what appeared to be a living space. Once again, he closed the gate behind them.

They stood still, with just their eyes surveying the spacious communal living area, divided into two alcoves. On the right, the walls echoed the same ruby-red hue as downstairs. There was a collection of puffy black leather couches surrounding a chrome coffee table, and a giant fake palm in the corner. An array of dog-eared fashion magazines and empty glasses lay on the well-used table.

In contrast to the dark sitting area, the alcove on the left was painted white with a continuous grey melamine counter that wrapped around the room. White plastic and chrome chairs sat scattered in a disorderly fashion. From the large window on this side of the room, Mbali could see some leafy treetops swaying. In the corner, there was a kettle and an array of mugs hanging from crude hooks, next to a steel sink. A small fridge hummed incessantly from under the counter. Items of colourful clothing lay haphazardly draped over the arms of the couches and on the kitchen work surface.

Directly in the middle of the airy room was a wide archway leading to a tunnel-like corridor. On both sides of the dark passageway, there was an open door, with a third closed door at the very end.

Baba Mthunzi raised his voice as he clapped to announce his arrival. "Girls! Girls! Come here and welcome some new friends!"

Almost immediately, well-proportioned figures swathed in colourful gowns and towelling head wraps began to appear from both doorways. Some of the girls made themselves comfortable on the couches, while others chose to lean against the walls as they tended to their nails. Most of the girls appeared to be in their early twenties with one or two possibly even in their thirties. There were 11 women in total, or 'girls' as Baba Mthunzi insisted on calling them. Some with neatly plaited braids and some with naturally short styles; some darker toned skin than others, but all equally as lovely in their individual right. For the two Mthethwa girls seeing a group of smiling female faces welcoming them into this strange place, offered a moment of relief.

Baba Mthunzi clapped his hands once more to get their undivided attention. "Girls, as you know Nandi was unwell, so her two daughters have asked me if they can work at my esteemed establishment."

Mbali felt her annoyance level rising. *Has he forgotten that he gave us no choice in the matter?*

"Well, I want you to treat these two new girls, Ayize and Mbali like your sisters. You must teach them how to treat our customers well," Baba Mthunzi wheezed as he took a deep breath in, "and most importantly, show them that if they are good to Baba, that Baba will be good to them." Just as he was turning to leave, he stopped and turned back to face everyone. "Also, I want you to help the new girls make a list of their essentials so that Patricia can do their shopping tomorrow."

Baba Mthunzi looked conceitedly at his new recruits. Then realising he had forgotten something particularly important.

"Ayize, you should feel flattered today because you will be doing your mother's job! It is hard work, but you will make many friends here." He pointed Ayize towards the room on the left of the passage. "This is your room."

Then he turned to Mbali. "As for you my Little Princess, you will be for my VIP Lounge. That's the most valuable part of my business, do you hear? So, I will expect a lot from you." With that, he gestured her towards the room on the right.

Mbali wanted to scream. *His Little Princess! His Little Princess! I don't want to be his anything!* She bit her tongue, unsure how much more of this she could swallow in silence.

"The girls in your rooms will teach you all you need to know. If you have any questions which the girls cannot answer," he paused for a moment as he looked at each of them, "then you come talk to me, or to Tau." Baba looked at the two Mthethwa girls, "Today is Sunday, so no work for anyone today, but you two will start this coming Friday."

He gave a half-hearted wave of the hand and left with the clang of the gate. For a moment, Ayize and Mbali stood in the communal living space under the scrutinising gaze of the other girls, but soon the chattering of introductions began.

CHAPTER SEVEN

The energetic dancing tune of Queen's cell-phone shook her from the champagne-induced deep sleep. Leaning over to retrieve her phone she read: 'UNKNOWN NUMBER', and then noticed the time was 7:02 AM!

Who in their right mind calls someone at this hour on a Sunday morning! Queen slid the phone under her pillow to drown out the now annoyingly harsh tune.

It was after 8:30 AM when she finally stirred again, turning over to lie on her back, she stretched her arms emitting a rather loud yawn. The room was still dark, so she pressed a button on the LCD panel that lay on the nightstand. The curtains began to open revealing a stunning sunny morning, and as the view widened, the sun rays hit the carpet, then the bed before finally making its way up her bare legs. The warmth was like a hug from the heavens. Queen comforted herself momentarily with a bloated feather pillow, smiling. "Oh, it is good to be alive!"

Rising from the bed, Queen moved her cell-phone to the nightstand. Then using her LCD panel once more, she engaged the local radio station before sauntering to the coolness of the marble stone bathroom. A spacious room of luxury with double sinks, a giant corner spa bath, as well as a rain shower enclosure for two. Queen began brushing her teeth, but before she could finish, her phone was blaring away again. Trying to rinse her mouth quickly, she managed to reach the phone in time to see 'UNKNOWN NUMBER' again. This time she answered.

"Hello, Queen speaking," she announced a little irked.

"Ahhh finally the queen is awake," a man's voice jested patronisingly. "I left you a message earlier which you probably haven't read yet, since I find myself still sitting here alone. Unless you just don't like me!" He chortled school-boyishly.

At first, Queen was unsure of who this annoyance was, but the remarkably happy and unrelenting, somewhat immature disposition soon gave the mystery away.

"Good morning Mathew," she said allowing her tone to soften, "and you are 100% correct! I have not yet looked at my phone this morning. As you can imagine, it turned out to be quite a late evening last night. Perhaps too many sips of champagne might have contributed to my slow rising." Queen was smiling before she even realised it.

Mathew laughed. "Well, now that you have enjoyed your beauty sleep, would you care to join me for brunch?" Without waiting for a response, he rambled on, "after all, I have been here for over an hour and a half, and I suspect the waitress thinks I have taken the adage of a 'bottomless coffee' as a personal challenge!"

A 'spontaneous brunch' is not what Queen had anticipated this morning, but she was rather hungry. Considering Mathew's ability to lift her spirits, she conceded. "Yes! I would love that!" With the cell phone locked between her ear and shoulder, Queen made a half-hearted attempt to make her bed. "Give me 30 minutes or so to get ready, if you don't mind waiting a little longer? I can join you at 9:30am?"

"It would be my pleasure to wait for you Queen," he said sincerely, before proceeding to tell her at which trendy café she could meet him.

Parking her silver sports convertible, supplied courtesy of Isaac M, Queen retrieved her Louis Vuitton handbag from the passenger seat. She pressed the button on her car key and with a piercing 'bleep' her 'sex-on-wheels' was secure, and she was tip-toeing her way towards the café, in her tan-coloured gladiator stilettos.

Queen spotted Mathew with his unruly wavy hair and a big smile from quite the distance. For some reason, she felt quite exposed walking towards him. Perhaps it was his concentrated stare. Unbeknown to her, the sun was filtering just perfectly through her white linen dress, silhouetting her figure. For this reason, Mathew could not break his intense stare and goofy grin.

This woman is breath-taking, he thought surreptitiously.

Hooking his sunglasses on the neckline of his surf-style t-shirt, Mathew stood to greet Queen with a kiss on both cheeks. Admiring her, he suddenly felt quite underdressed in his khakis and flip-flops.

"Good morning again," said Queen, slipping her silky long Peruvian weave behind her bare shoulders, as she perched her sunglasses atop her head.

Mathew could not stop grinning, to the point that he was beginning to feel ridiculous. "Yes, indeed good morning again! I sincerely apologise for the early wake-up call, as usual, I wasn't thinking."

Queen could hear the sincerity in his voice. This entire experience summarised who Mathew was. An over-exuberant ordinarily good guy, with no airs and graces. She concluded that he must hold some presence in business otherwise Kgabu would not keep him so close. As drawn to Mathew as Queen was, she was unsure of whether he would be accepting of her lifestyle, however, if he chose not to ask, then she chose not to divulge such information.

The 09:30am brunch rolled to 01:00pm, then to 02:00pm and the waitress appeared to be tired of continually interrupting their conversation to ask if there was anything further they required.

Finally, Mathew cheerfully suggested, "Perhaps it is time to free up this table for some afternoon coffee drinkers."

Queen agreed and thanked him for a wonderfully impromptu outing. After Mathew settled the bill, with what must have been a hefty tip for the now profusely grateful waitress, they left the café heading towards Queen's car.

"I'd love to see you again Queen, perhaps when I get back from Ghana later in the week may I call you?" He asked.

Queen was elated, "Sure! Mathew, I would like that a great deal."

They reached Queen's car. With her hand placed lightly on his upper arm, she gave him a friendly kiss on the cheek. "Thank you again for brunch, and now for also walking me to my car."

"No problemo!" Mathew replied, "Just going to be a very looooong walk back to mine," and with that, he pressed the button on his car key. The lights of a new model, top of the range German luxury 4x4 parked right behind her, flashed amber.

"Oh, you are so silly!" She exclaimed, laughing.

He grinned back raising his thick eyebrows, "I couldn't help myself!"

Mathew clicked the car door closed, as Queen settled in behind the wheel, before starting the growling engine and driving off.

Esjay C. Moore

Watching her car roll from sight, Mathew thought to himself, *I am going to have to up my game if I am going to impress this woman next time. I don't believe I have measured up to her standards of expectation thus far.*

CHAPTER EIGHT

In the VIP girls' quarters, there were eight beds, four on each wall. Next to each was a personal locker for them to keep their valuables. Mbali was to be the sixth girl in this section. She had a choice of the three remaining beds which were all at the front of the room, closest to the door.

She learned that the mysterious door at the end of the long passage, was the washroom consisting of four shower cubicles, four basins with mirrors and four toilets, of which usually at least one was not working. Mbali felt a level of resentment directed towards her when one of the other girls sarcastically passed a sly comment to another: "at least the farm girls will now have hot running water to wash with." Mbali could not argue that point, so chose to ignore the cynical tone.

Mbali sat on the end of the bed not sure what to do. She watched the others continuing with their hair, and ironing and whatever else they did on a Sunday morning. She quietly sat listening to them chattering away amidst the activities.

Just then one of the other girls sat on the bed next to Mbali's. "My name is Zanele," said the pleasant-looking girl in the vermillion-coloured gown.

"Hello," Mbali replied, "I'm not sure what I should be doing. Perhaps I should check my sister?"

Zanele gave a little frown, "You can do that, but understand that us VIP girls are different to those girls, and we don't often mingle with them."

"But why? They are just young women like us!"

"Mbali, when we start working, you will understand, and your sister might become a different person to you," Zanele said firmly. "I will take care of you just as I would of my own sister. Now let's make your list as Baba has asked for, then afterwards you can go visit Ayize, okay?"

Mbali nodded.

While generating the list of deodorant, lip gloss, moisturiser, and the like, Mbali learnt that Zanele had been here for three years already. She was from the Eastern Cape and had run away from her abusive stepfather, and unfortunately right into the clutches of Baba Mthunzi. At first, she found it difficult but learned that if she followed the rules, it was in fact, better than her abusive life at home.

Zanele stopped writing for a moment to look at Mbali. "Now for your hair? Do you want a wig or braids or weaves or do you just want to keep it natural?"

Mbali touched her short curly hair, wondering what was wrong with it and answered, "I don't understand? I just want to keep it like this."

"Well you could, the patrons might like this way seeing as it is so … Ummm, undeveloped. I think you should give it some thought for the future. For now, we will just comb some oil through to give it some strength." Zanele scribbled on a scrap of paper. "Who knows you might want to grow it out natural and put a nice long weave." She smiled.

Just then the inaudible utterances of a man could be heard in the living area.

"Yay, it's Tau! He has brought us our usual Sunday lunch!" Zanele announced, grabbing Mbali by the hand and tugging her up off the bed. "Come let's get some pizza to eat! First ones get the best pieces!"

"Ayize, are you doing ok?" Mbali asked while standing in the queue for pizza.

"Yes, my sister, I am okay," Ayize said as she helped herself to a slice of pizza. This type of food was such a treat for the Mthethwa girls. So much so that they only had pizza once in a blue moon when Mama sent money to Gogo. It was an exciting time for the children to open the square pizza box, to choose the cheesiest slice of Margherita. Gogo used to tease that she was the oldest so she would make her selection first, so they better not say which one they wanted, or else she would take it. Then the children would laugh and eat until their little bellies ached. Of course, Gogo never seemed to choose the best slice for fear she would break their eager little hearts.

"Mbali, ..." Ayize hesitated momentarily, "I have decided to sleep in Mama's old bed so that I can feel closer to her."

Mbali could already hear the sadness in Ayize's voice. She hugged her, then looked her in the eyes, "We are here together, just for one-year Ayize! Please be strong! We can only do this together!"

An hour later, the 13 girls had devoured all the pizzas and were ready to spend their Sunday afternoon lazing within the confines of the sun-speckled courtyard. Under the watchful eye of Tau, they headed down the dark stairwell with a collection of towels and the latest bunch of magazines to read.

From the courtyard enclosure, the booming sounds of music coming from the Tavern were significantly amplified and competed with the sounds of people laughing and singing. There was also a delicious smell of food cooking, which both Ayize and Mbali noticed.

"That's the 'Weekend Shishanyama Special', it smells delicious right!" Said Zanele matter-of-factly. "The Tavern is famous for this, but we only have leftovers when there are some. We must just hope those greedy pigs don't eat it all!" She laughed loudly with the others.

The next morning Patricia entered the girls' section to collect the bed linen and do a general check. Introducing herself to the newcomers, she took a measuring tape from her pocket.

"I need to get your measurements to order you some working clothes." The girls handed Patricia their lists of essentials, which she skimmed through to see if anything was amiss. With a nod of her head, she walked to the doorway, then rung the intercom for Tau to let her out.

By 04:00pm the working girls were prepping themselves for their evening shift. The usual working hours were six to eleven, Monday to Thursday; and six until the last patron in their section left on Fridays and Saturdays. The girls did not earn a wage, but they did accept tips, and how much they received was entirely dependent on what they were prepared to offer. Baba Mthunzi's excuse for not paying is that he provided the personal essentials within a limit, free accommodation with laundry service and three daily meals.

CHAPTER NINE

The cold Cape Town wind howled wildly as Kgabu and Queen stepped off the plane. En route from the airport, the driver was briefed to deliver Queen at the mall before heading off to Kgabu's 10:30am meeting in the Central Business District.

Queen mulled over the timing quietly, calculating that she would have five productive hours of shopping before the driver would collect her again. Kgabu, held out his Black Card to Queen, and just as she attempted to take it from him, he quickly snapped it back cheekily. "Remember to include a little something special for me!"

Queen pouted exaggeratedly like the cat that almost had the cream. "When have I ever forgotten about you?" Her pout broke into a wicked smile, "besides, I already have something in mind," she said with a teasing wink, followed by a quick peck on his cheek. She quickly seized the card playfully from his fingers and escaped through the open door.

The wind seemed even angrier at this spot, so Queen wrapped her oversized tweed jacket closed to keep herself warm. Adjusting her scarf over her long hair, she stepped out the car onto the cobblestone verge. Blowing a quick kiss to Kgabu,

Queen was soon swept up in the current of the morning shopping crowd.

Kgabu watched her walk away holding her headscarf to prevent it from being blown into the gusty wind. He watched until he could no longer catch a glimpse of her. Queen possessed an attractive liquidity in the way she walked, her body swayed smoothly, like a panther with each stalking step. Soon she was swallowed up by the wall of shoppers.

"Ahhhhh, later my lovely," Kgabu purred quietly, as he considered what delights he would indulge in later. Perhaps tonight would be his night.

Later that evening, once back at the boutique hotel, the inviting scent of vanilla candles filled the luxurious corner apartment. The ceiling lights were dimmed slightly, highlighting the expansive view of the cityscape twinkling like stars in the purple-grey haze of Cape Town's dusk.

The hot steam was rising from Kgabu's still wet body when he exited the bathroom. The fluffy white towel with the decorative gold hotel emblem was tucked in safely around his hips. Entering the bedroom, he stopped in awe.

There was Queen, perched upon the button-punched velvet ottoman. Waiting! Her body was pinched tightly by an emerald green satin corset with black boning, and lace-edged cups, from which the curves of her full breasts presented themselves flawlessly.

She stood slowly, revealing thigh-high fishnet stockings, and dangerous-looking black stilettos. Queen turned her back to him so he could absorb the wonder of her curvaceous perfection. Raising one hand after the other, she adjusted her elbow-length black satin gloves one at a time. She glanced at Kgabu from over her shoulder to ensure he was watching her, before provocatively bending down even further to pick something up. It was a riding crop!

Eager to feel her perfection under his hands, Kgabu took two steps towards her, but she spun around to face him.

"Did I say you could move?" She asked firmly. Her legs positioned slightly apart, as she began to bend the crop in her hands.

Kgabu immediately stood motionless, "Erm... No, you didn't," he responded cautiously.

Her stare was infallible, "'No, I didn't' WHO?" Queen taunted in a somewhat aggressive manner, lightly slapping the crop's tip of folded leather against her palm.

Kgabu looked shocked, almost embarrassed. Typically he was the one making the demands, both in business and in the bedroom, but now he felt confused, yet exhilarated at the same time. This was a side of Queen he had never seen before, and it aroused him.

"No, you didn't ... Madame Queen?" He answered a little unsure if this was the response she wished to hear.

Queen slinked towards him like a sleek cat ready to pounce.

"Good boy!" She praised him in a patronising tone. Staring directly into his eyes while holding his jaw firmly with her one hand, she placed the tip of the crop on his lips with the other.

"I only want you to talk when I ask you to. Do you understand me?" She said sternly in a breathy tone.

Kgabu nodded in agreement, not sure he even recognised this intriguing, possibly dangerous creature in front of him. Releasing her determined grip on his jaw she dragged the folded leather tip down to his goateed chin, then slowly down his neck to pause on his masculine chest. She stared him in the eyes like an unpredictable jaguar, then steadily moved the crop down to the tightly tucked towel-line.

"You have an impressive body." She remarked. Her gloved fingertips marvelling at his defined form.

Kgabu realised she was probably testing him for a response. Biting his now dry lip, he stared straight ahead, trying to ignore the thumping of his

heart that was beating out of his chest. *Breathe!*
Just Breathe! He reminded himself.

Slowly Queen walked around him, keeping the
crop firmly on his skin. When returning to her
starting point, she pulled the towel from where it
was safely tucked. It fell in a dishevelled damp heap
on the floor, revealing the fact that Kgabu was
suitably aroused by this activity. Queen expected
nothing less of Kgabu, not only was his proud
phallus perfect in proportion, but substantial in
size.

Queen peered deep into Kgabu's eyes. "You are
well-endowed," she said approvingly. He smiled,
almost embarrassed by the compliment and at the
same time tempted to thank her for noticing.

Stepping around him once again, Queen
lowered the crop, little by little. Then without
warning: Whack! She flicked her wrist quickly to
land a stinging slap of the flexible crop against his
bare buttock.

Kgabu flinched and gave a little moan. Queen
smiled wickedly.

"Do you want me to do that again?" She asked.

"Yes, please ... Madame Queen." He uttered.

With that, she gave his other buttock a clean
stinging slap of the folded leather tip. This time it
was even harder. The welts were already rising
under his skin. Queen pulled the sensible-looking
hotel chair away from the writing desk.

"Sit!" She instructed him firmly. He sat feeling the stinging even more so now. He liked it.

Restraining his wrists and ankles to the wooden chair with shiny satin bands, Queen intended to taunt and tantalise Kgabu further. She stood before him and placed the red sole of her stiletto against his bare privates. She leaned in closer towards him increasing the pressure against him. He moaned a little as he felt the pressure bearing down on him, but at the same time, the rounded curves of her breasts were teasingly suspended in front of his face.

Queen took Kgabu's ear lobe between the warmth of her full lips and sucked it firmly. Taking the lobe between her teeth, she gave it a little bite to get his attention. His skin came alive with a myriad of bumps. He was completely turned on!

"I am going to make you beg for my mercy," Queen whispered closely in his ear, before giving it a lick with her wet tongue.

Kgabu barely heard what she said, for he noticed her black satin and lace panties were crotchless. Realising she had revealed herself purposely to him, his parched mouth now ached to taste her. Nearing the peak of his craving, Kgabu tried to reach his hand to touch this captivating creature but did so without success.

"Please!" He begged desperately, "please put me out my misery Madame Queen! I will do anything for you, just please!" He pleaded sincerely.

Queen smiled. She knew she had finally broken his usually calm and collected resolve. She straightened her posture and turned to position her rounded satin and lace buttocks on his bare lap. With skin against skin, she gyrated slowly against his nakedness. Unable to take her in his yearning hands, Kgabu was driven by his passion. He gently bit her smooth back and shoulder, allowing her to rock herself so close into position. *So very close. Just a little more*, he begged silently.

Then she stopped.

Queen glimpsed back at him. With a mischievous smile, "I think you ought to wait to enjoy your dessert after supper." She teased.

Kgabu let out a loud laugh of agonising disbelief, "Ah Queen! I would never believe you would be so cruel as to leave me hanging!"

Queen tittered playfully. "Well, I wouldn't say hanging exactly!" She laughed mischievously, "think of this as just the prelude to the rest of the evening."

Sitting at the hotel's cocktail bar, now respectfully dressed, and awaiting their table, it was undeniable that Kgabu was now wholly smitten with Queen after their recent, most stimulating, activities. Although they had become intimately acquainted over the last three months, Queen had not yet allowed him to fully indulge in the most intimate of carnal pleasures. Now he could not stop smiling at her, touching her, and wishing for the evening to hurry; yet at the same time enjoying the excruciating wait for his promised dessert. *Tonight is definitely the night!* He smiled.

Just then, Kgabu received a call. "Sorry Queen, I have to take this!" He apologised, as he stood to leave the bar for the privacy of the foyer. Queen sipped on her cool Cosmopolitan, to distract from the fact that she knew he had left to take a call from his wife. It was not unusual for her to call him when he travelled, and Queen would never fault her for that. Staring into her crimson-coloured cocktail, Queen was transfixed in deep thought of how it must be to have a person who cared about your well-being. Deep in her moment of contemplation, she did not notice that someone other than Kgabu had claimed the seat next to her.

"Evening beautiful!" The stranger said.

At first glance, this man was about 28, well-dressed. He leant against the bar, appearing to have already imbibed one too many drinks. Queen placed the long-stemmed glass back on the glossy wooden bar-top.

"Good evening," she responded politely, glancing briefly towards the door to see if Kgabu was in sight.

"Well? Aren't you going to tell me your name?" He slurred aggressively.

Queen turned back to the stranger. "I am here with someone." She attempted to explain civilly.

He laughed obnoxiously, looking back to his pair of red-faced friends sitting at the booth in the dimly-lit corner. They appeared to encourage him further.

"Fine. Normally I am more polished in my approach, but since you are under pressure, I will make this quick!" He continued, "my friends and I think you are a pretty decent looking hooker." A hint of vindictiveness entered his tenor. "Since we are staying here tonight, we would like to invite you to join us for some fun."

Queen was humiliated and hoped the barman did not overhear this conversation. "I am not a ... a 'hooker' as you put it! I would appreciate it if you would just leave me alone," she implored emphatically.

"Ooooooooooh so you're a fiery one too, eh? Just what we like!" He provoked her further. "Look we saw you with grandpa, and we are pretty sure us three could offer you a better time."

That was the final straw, Queen picked up her evening bag and slid herself from her barstool. As she hurriedly made for the doorway, Kgabu was also returning. She skimmed past him not sure whether to cry from embarrassment or anger. "I'm sorry Kgabu, I believe I have lost my appetite."

Confused and not understanding the circumstances that led to this moment, Kgabu followed her to the elevator.

"What's the matter, Queen?" He asked sincerely, as he pushed the button for the top floor.

"It's nothing," she replied refusing to look him in the eyes.

"It must be something Queen? Is it that I took the call from my wife?"

The elevator purred consistently making its way ever higher.

"No, it's never you." Queen finally looked at him with tears welling in her eyes. To be honest, Kgabu, lately, I have come to understand that I need to make changes in my life. For my self-preservation, I have to, but I don't know how to. I feel trapped."

Kgabu pulled her tightly to him and wrapped his arms around her petiteness. "I'm not sure what has brought this on so suddenly, but if you want to talk about it, you can always do so with me Queen." His voice was gentle and caring. "You should know that I would never stand in the way of you living the life you want."

Exhaling a deep sigh, Queen felt his calmness seeping into her soul. "Kgabu, I think it's almost time. I just don't know how to go about it," she replied in a faint voice.

Still holding her tightly as they reached their floor, Kgabu held a suspicion that this might have been spurred on by a particular person of interest. That being, none other than his friend and employee: Mathew Tillman.

God forbid that it is Mathew, not sure I could cope having Queen involved with someone so 'close to home!' He quietly considered the possibility.

They walked in contemplative silence to the door, and as they stepped into the entrance, Kgabu offered some reassurance. "Queen, I always knew that having the pleasure of your company was a temporary arrangement."

"Thank you Kgabu for being so understanding," she said appreciatively. "It is just that I am re-evaluating my life, and I need to find myself again."

Removing his necktie, Khabu half-heartedly browsed the 'Room Service Menu' that lay on the table.

"You are worth far more than being kept as a prize Queen. Your life is what you dream to make of it, but if you ever need advice or assistance, you can always call me. No strings attached! Please know that."

Queen was quiet. She was not afraid of Kgabu. It was the devil himself that repetitively forced her to her knees that she feared most. Her 'liberator', disguised as an influential politician. He held the key to the exit door.

CHAPTER TEN

The group of girls made their way tentatively down the dimly lit steps towards the ominous black door. Mbali and Ayize had not seen the Tavern since they arrived almost a week before, but tonight was Friday and so this evening they began their work.

At precisely six o'clock, Tau opened the black-painted door leading from the hidden corridor to the Tavern. Immediately there was an assault on the senses, not just from the thumping noise, but the odour of alcohol, fried food, and cheap cologne. The rowdy Friday night festivities were in full swing. The crowd of drunken guests were laughing their week's woes away with colleagues and friends.

One by one the 'Tavern Girls' dressed in their red hot-pants, bright-white sneakers and skimpy white vests confidently entered the working area. The patrons hooted and cheered in appreciation as Tau directed the girls one-by-one through the doorway. Mbali grabbed for Ayize's arm as she passed.

"Ayize, be strong!" Without replying Ayize slipped through into the enthusiastic crowd.

The VIP girls stood patiently, all dressed in short black body-con dresses and cheap black strappy high-heels. It had taken the last three days for Mbali to learn to walk in these shoes, and even now she tottered precariously with every step. Moments later Tau directed them up the chrome stairway to a glass-enclosed mezzanine level.

In comparison to the ground level tavern, the VIP Lounge was plush and comfortable. Thick-piled red carpets dulled the drumming noise from downstairs. Sleek black leather tub-chairs and glitzy glass tables edged with chrome were distributed in orderly groups about the room. A long bar lined the one wall with an array of bottles and glasses neatly arranged on glass shelves. A man standing behind the bar was introduced to Mbali as "Vusi the Barman".

Apart from Vusi, there were five other well-dressed men seated around one of the tables playing cards and talking to Baba Mthunzi as he hunched over them. The seasoned VIP girls immediately flocked towards the cigar-smoke cloud, draping themselves provocatively over the arms of the chairs, cooing over the men eager to show their wealth through the size of their tips.

"Oh, Gentlemen! I have a surprise for you all tonight! This lovely young girl is my 'Little Princess'," Baba Mthunzi proudly announced while placing Mbali front and centre with his nicotine tainted hands on her slender shoulders. "I want you to be patient with her as it is her first night working here at the VIP Lounge."

At first, being on display was an awkward experience for Mbali, but the VIP girls happily shared their knowledge and suggestions with her during the week. Being as bright as she was, it did not take long before she was fetching and carrying expensive drinks to the paternal patrons.

The teasing flirtations and brushing of hands against her body were utterly foreign to Mbali, but when she saw the generosity of these men, she quickly learnt the art of faking an encouraging smile. The more the patrons drank, the more they tipped. The more they tipped, the more they believed they had the right to be even more obscene.

Occasionally, when passing behind the gentlemen, Mbali would take the opportunity to peer down to the tavern below to look for Ayize. Surprisingly, she seemed to be having fun, laughing and joking with the patrons. It may have been as instructed by the girls, but it was hard for Mbali to say from this angle.

As the evening progressed, more groups of smiling people entered the tavern, and a few more entered the VIP Lounge dressed in staid business attire. It appeared that this was a convenient stop after work and before loitering home on a Friday night. While seating new guests just after 11:00pm, Mbali could not help noticing that Ayize was gone. She walked near the chrome railing and glass wall to try another angle from above, but to no avail. Ayize was nowhere!

Panicked, Mbali approached Zanele, who was currently perched on the lap of a chubby man wearing a bowtie. His lumpy body rippled in waves with each laugh as he lecherously drooled over her like a giant dog in the height of a Durban summer.

Leaning in, Mbali whispered frantically in her ear. "Zanele! I can't see Ayize downstairs! She is gone!"

Zanele rolled her eyes at Mbali as she pushed her away. "She is working that's all! It's normal, but she will make good money, so don't worry so much."

Mbali was surprised that 'working Zanele' was far less empathic to the girl she knew beyond the black door.

Unfortunately, Zanele's explanation did nothing to ease Mbali's alarm for her sister. After serving the last drinks for the night, the girls wished their generous patrons a pleasant evening. Then they were rounded-up by Tau and shepherded back to their quarters. Mbali noticed Ayize was still absent on the ascent to their quarters.

Mbali pushed her way towards Tau and grabbed his elbow to get his attention. "Tau? My sister, Ayize? Where is she?" Mbali demanded.

"Don't worry! She is not feeling well, so I sent her to see Patricia. She should be upstairs already," Tau replied dismissively.

Mbali entered the Tavern Girls room on the left. She saw Ayize laying quietly on the bed with her back to the door.

Mbali hurried towards the bed. "Ayize! Are you ok?" She asked as she sat on the side of the bed.

There was no response. Mbali leaned over her sister so she could see her face. Her dark eyes appeared distant, staring into space. "Ayize, what is wrong? What happened?" Mbali asked with a trembling voice.

Ayize grabbed Mbali's hand and pulled her down to enfold herself within the protective embrace of her younger sister. The minutes ticked for what seemed like hours before Mbali spoke again. "Ayize, my sister you must tell me what is wrong."

Tears had formed in Ayize's eyes and trickled quietly down her cheeks. Knowing that she needed to tell her sister if not just to warn her. In a small voice, Ayize began to explain how she did what she was told to do.

She was friendly with the customers. She even excepted the invitation to make more money and went with the man to a bedroom behind the black door. Patricia was there waiting outside, where she wrote some details in a book. Ayize explained how the man placed his hands where no man had done so before.

She told him, "NO!" and even pushed him off, but this did not help. He raped her until she bled. Afterwards, while she lay huddled on the bed in the dimly lit room, he thanked her and put R100 next to her. The next thing she knew Patricia brought her upstairs to the shower, explaining that it was that way the first time, and then put her to bed with some tablets.

Mbali's face was now wet with the tears she shed quietly listening to how she failed to protect her sister. She was angry at herself for blindly getting them into this mess, and now Ayize was paying the price. That night Mbali slept with Ayize on the small bed. Two souls with innocence lost, as they now realised what lay before them.

The next evening, and many more evenings after that, Ayize robotically performed the routine expectations. Her mantra before the work shift began, was: "It's one night closer to leaving." Each of the mornings following those nights, she was quiet and withdrawn, until the person that Mbali once knew as her bubbly sister was a distant memory. Ayize had surrendered herself to a shell of her former self.

Some weeks later it became evident to Mbali, that some of the money Ayize was earning was going towards drugs issued by Patricia as a side-hustle. Nonchalantly, Zanele explained that succumbing to drugs was not an uncommon problem for the Tavern Girls, as it was their only means of coping mentally.

To protect their wounded souls, they gave their hard-earned money straight back to the same 'machine' that kept them prisoner. Mbali now understood why they never heard from their mother again. There were drugs to lighten the mood, to make them more acquiescent to the sexual favours; and others to lessen the after-effects of guilt and diminish the distaste for what they endured.

As much as Mbali tried to stop Ayize from using the drugs, she also understood why it was necessary. Before long Ayize's grip weakened, and she slipped into the abyss, while Mbali could do nothing but feel an immense level of guilt.

Such things did not happen for the VIP Girls. For the most part, the VIP Girls were treated well only having to endure some occasional opportunistic groping. By comparison, they did little to earn their generous tips from their usual wealthy patrons.

Mbali stood at the doorway to the Tavern Girls room watching Ayize. It finally dawned on her why Zanele had said on the first day that Ayize may become a different person, and why the two groups chose not to mingle with each other. Right before Mbali's eyes, her sister had transformed into an unrecognisable person with bottomless black eyes.

There was nothing Mbali could do about it, except to keep her resolve even stronger.

The first anniversary of their 'contract' at Baba Mthunzi's was nearing, and Mbali's spirit began to lift. As much as the girls informed Mbali that there was no way they would be leaving, she hung on the hope that she and Ayize would one day, as broken as they now were, would walk from the building with their shoeboxes of earnings. She longed to see their home amongst the hills again, to hug Gogo and laugh at Mandla's silliness.

Just as the other girls had said, the 365th day at Mthunzi's came and went. Life continued as it had done for the last twelve months. Mbali pleaded and begged and cried in angry frustration, but it fell on deaf ears. She knew now that there never was a contract, there was never a year of working for the two of them. They had willingly handed themselves over to Baba Mthunzi. This imprisonment was their fate, and there was nothing Mbali could do to change it now. She wept silently.

CHAPTER ELEVEN

As promised Mathew called from Ghana to let Queen know he was back late on Wednesday evening. He had arranged to have the day off from the office on Thursday, to spend with her.

Walking across the marbled foyer, Queen greeted the building's concierge, whom she knew as Mr Slade. As usual, he tipped his hat to her with a courteous greeting before opening the door by the shiny brass handle.

"Miss Queen, your car is waiting over there." He gestured her towards Mathew's freshly washed 4x4.

"Ahhh thank you Mr Slade, and you enjoy your day," she said merrily, to which he smiled and wished her the same.

Nearing the vehicle, Queen expected to see Mathew, but it was a younger figure who exited the driver's side and made his way around to open the backseat door for her.

"Good morning Ma'am, I'm Khaya. I'm Mr Tillman's driver." He said with a magnificent smile and a spirited glint in his eyes.

Queen removed her taupe-coloured Fedora as she approached the car door. "Thank you Khaya," she said making herself comfortable inside.

"Any idea where you are taking me this morning?" She asked as the car began to navigate from the collection zone.

"Oh, I'm afraid that is top secret ma'am! Mr Tilman has sworn me to secrecy!" Khaya responded, then added jokingly, "You wouldn't want me to jeopardise this top-secret mission, now would you?"

"No of course not!" she responded realising this young man was both confident and well-educated. "How long have you been driving for Mr Tillman, Khaya?" Queen asked.

He looked at her in the rear-view mirror, and said, "Well it's a long story, which I would prefer not to bore you with Ma'am."

She admired his beautiful bright eyes with the most enviable eyelashes she had ever seen. "Well, maybe another time then?" Feeling a little awkward with his referring to her as Ma'am, she continued, "and Khaya, please call me Queen. Ma'am makes me sound far too old."

"I have strict instructions, Ma'am," he replied.

Khaya quietly admired the beautiful young woman sitting behind him. *Apart from her obvious beauty, there is something about her that makes her incredibly attractive.* He studied her in his rear-view mirror, *somehow, she possesses a poorly disguised vulnerability.*

"Well, your boss isn't here, and after all, I am sure he would want me to feel comfortable." She responded confidently.

"Yes, Miss Queen," Khaya said smiling cheekily.

"Oh, my word!" She exclaimed throwing her head back slowly onto the black-leather headrest, "Khaya, you're as sassy as your boss!"

There it is! Khaya thought. *The glimmer of girlishness hidden behind a highly polished façade.* He smiled broadly.

They both shared a laugh, before Khaya replied, "it's not normally like this Ma'am, I believe Mr Tillman might wish to make an extra good impression today."

Queen smiled as she peered out the window, wondering to herself. *What is with these men lately? Not only do they all seem so refreshingly high-spirited, but they are so appealing.* She quietly pondered what Khaya's 'long story' could be.

The car growled along the freeway, taking the Eastern Bypass, Queen considered that if Mathew wished to impress her, what could possibly be near the industrial area of Germiston to do so. It was all very mysterious, and now she was thankful that she had decided to tone down her attire for 'Mr I'm-So-Casual'.

For today, Queen selected her favourite skinny designer-label jeans, with a crisp white cotton blouse, pointy-toed kitten heels and carried a fawn-coloured wool jacket just in case. Of course, the outfit was incomplete until she added her chunky gold jewellery and oversized sunglasses.

I wonder what he has planned? Queen quietly peered out the window, knowing that Khaya would not relinquish the details even if she asked.

A few minutes later the car turned in towards the small private airport.

"Ahhh I get it! I'm going on a sightseeing tour by air!" Queen announced.

Khaya looked at her again through the rear-view mirror. "I would expect something a little more exciting from Matt ... I mean, Mr Tillman." He hoped she had not realised his stumble.

Queen did not miss the near miswording, and it dawned on her that Khaya was probably not the 'driver', but rather someone closer, with whom Mathew was on a first-name basis. She smiled and wisely chose to keep this opinion to herself; she considered the alternatives for being at an airport.

"Well, it better not be parachuting because I can tell you right now that is NOT happening!!" She exclaimed quite emphatically.

The car rolled slowly towards a silver-black coloured helicopter. Then came to a complete halt.

Mathew was standing nearby, nervously waiting for his guest. As Queen stepped from the car, she thanked Khaya.

"The pleasure is all mine, Miss Queen ... Ma'am," He replied with a dimpled smile.

With armed stretched open, Mathew walked towards Queen, greeting her with a warm hug and a simple peck on the cheek. Mathew air-punched a thumbs-up to Khaya, before turning towards the waiting chopper.

Mathew took Queen's hand and led her towards the impressive machine. "I'm so happy to see you again," he said as he guided her into the front passenger seat, "and you look lovely as usual."

"Surely you are not planning on flying this are you?" Queen asked noticing there was no pilot in the vicinity.

Mathew chuckled, "Well actually, I am most definitely planning to!" He buckled up her safety harness, "besides, it's my proverbial boy-toy which I don't get enough downtime to enjoy these days!"

Before securely clicking the door closed, Mathew handed Queen the headset, asking her to turn off her cell-phone, then walked around the bulbous glass nose of the helicopter to the pilot's door. Queen looked a little surprised and somewhat terrified.

Soon they were all harnessed up. Headsets on and the rotor blades above were whirring rapidly. After a few flicks of switches, the go-ahead was given to ascend into the air. Not being fond of heights, Queen gripped her seat tightly as she watched Khaya waving from below, fading from view with every second. Minutes later they had cleared the low airspace of the city limits and were making their way through the clear blue sky.

"How are you with heights, Queen?"

"Nice of you to ask now!" Queen replied half in jest and half in terror.

Mathew chortled. "Don't worry so much. Don't you know you are in good hands!" Soon Mathew was relaying the story of how he had gotten the 'bug' to fly from his British grandfather. Soon enough the fear began to dissipate, and Queen was finally able to relax sufficiently to enjoy the ever-changing scenery skimming below.

She had to admit Mathew certainly looked sexy and more of a man's man than she had noticed before.

After 30 minutes, the hustling cityscape morphed into a natural terrain, and Mathew pointed out markers of places and buildings. None of which seemed familiar to Queen, besides there was only one terrain she was interested in. It began with an "M" and ended with "athew". Queen smiled sheepishly.

"Where are we?" She asked through the headset.

"We are heading towards Limpopo." He said turning to smile at her. "Right! I think it is time you try to fly this silver bird Queen!" He announced.

"Oh No! No! No! I seriously don't think so!!!" She said raising her arms in a mad panic.

Mathew was beaming. "Don't be scared, it's easier than you think! Here let me guide your hand." He placed his hand over hers as she firmly gripped the cyclic controller.

It was the longest ten minutes of Queen's life, as she moved from panicked, to being petrified then finally to being amazed. Closing in on their destination, Mathew took back full the control for the last stretch.

"Queen, before we get side-tracked by people once we land," Mathew paused momentarily to focus on manoeuvring the helicopter cyclic, as the ground rose to meet the 'skids' below. "I'm leaving for Ghana on Sunday." He glanced at her to gauge her initial response while he continued to explain, "Unfortunately, this was arranged a few weeks back, before I met you. I will be gone for at least three months as I have to set up an office there."

Queen feigned a gracious smile but felt her heart sink just a little.

The incessant shuddering of the rotor blades above slowly came to a halt.

The private game lodge was ultra-luxurious. Granted, Queen had been treated to luxury private game lodges before, but nothing like this. Even she, who was now quite used to decadences in life, was overwhelmed as she beheld her opulent surrounds.

Lavishly decorated in creams, golds, and beiges with a hint of azure blue, the elegant suite was close to 100m2 in size. But it was the seamless 360-degree view of the wild bush and river, which the glass-enclosed suite offered, that was indeed breathtaking.

"Queen, come you have to experience this." Mathew opened the cascading glass doors allowing Queen to step out onto the deck. The buzzing sounds of insects living in the Acacia trees, and the distinct smell of the wild grasses, always felt like home to Queen. She stood silently, admiring the view of the flowing river from the deck.

Mathew handed Queen a flute of cold champagne, which she stood holding, astonished by her surrounds.

"I hope you like this spot? It's one of my favourite places which I wanted to share with you." She felt her heart pounding as he slipped his hand around her tiny waist. Not sure whether it was the exhilaration of the over-the-top experience, the sip of champagne or Mathew's arm around her, Queen felt her knees weaken.

"Oh, my goodness Mathew, what is not to like?" She exclaimed, then more seriously added, "but I'm afraid I wasn't expecting a night away, so I haven't brought anything with me."

"Not to worry, Queen. You will find the bedroom and the bathroom furnished with everything you will be needing." Mathew was beginning to sound rather proud of himself, "and one more thing, but I'm sorry there is no cell-phone reception here at all. It's one of the reasons I choose this particular suite." At this given moment, her cell-phone was the last thing on her mind.

"For now, we can just chill, perhaps a little swim, a few drinks, and a light lunch, then later I have arranged for a private chef to prepare our dinner, while we take a game drive."

Queen wandered through the open-plan space to the bedroom area, Mathew walked behind her outlining his plans for their getaway together. "How does dinner on the deck sound?" He asked.

Queen was looking at the array of clothes and shoes, provided for just one evening, and even the finer details of a bikini and makeup remover.

"Perfect Mathew. It's all perfect." Queen realised that if he was aiming to impress as Khaya had said, then he had certainly done that. Seeing all these items neatly lined up, somehow brought back the essentials lists she and the VIP girls would make once a month. Unfortunately, having made the connection with her memories Queen felt a twinge of agitation and swiftly reminded herself that this held an entirely different intention.

The private game drive was spectacular.

"Did you pay to have all the wildlife make a special appearance today?" Queen joked.

"Sure did! Just wait until you see the sunrise I have planned," Mathew joked in return.

The sun was now setting below the bushy horizon, and the crispness of a late winters' evening was creeping into Queen's bones. The fact that they were hidden under a blanket in an open-top Land Rover did little to keep them warm. Nearing their private suite close to the river's edge, the delicious aroma of a hearty supper, professionally prepared in their absence lured them ever closer. The warm lights twinkled, bathing the opulent glass enclosure in a milky way of stars, guiding them down the secluded driveway.

Once inside, Queen opted for a shower before supper. She stood naked in the shower appreciating the warmth of the water droplets falling on her now dusty dry skin. For a moment, she quietly enjoyed the soft water settling lightly on her face. She recalled the humid summer days of her youth when the late afternoon tropical rain showers would beckon the valley's children to gather outside to cool down. Lost in her memories, she was startled when two hands touched her bare shoulders, sliding down her arms to her hips. Instinctively, she placed her hands on his to stop them from wandering further.

"Do you mind if I share the shower with you?" Mathew asked softly.

"I couldn't have suggested a better idea," she said turning to face him, his hands rested on the rounded convex of her buttocks.

Looking at her bright eyes, he felt an urge to kiss her. Bowing down slightly he kissed her softly on her full lips; they were exactly as he imagined: soft and sweet. She tasted like ripe strawberries.

Easing him closer to her under the cascading water, Queen reciprocated. Their kisses were gentle at first then growing increasingly hungrier and more passionate. The hot steam filled the double cubicle as they explored each other for the first time. The intimate attraction for each other was mutual and honest. Soon damp bodies moved from the shower to the bedroom, entwined in an embrace of heated desire.

After a session of intense lovemaking, the adoring new lovers dressed in the plush towelling gowns. Anything else would just be more complicated to remove should they wish. Making themselves comfortable on the snug outdoor couch next to the glowing log firepit, they casually indulged in the delicious oxtail supper that the chef expertly prepared for them earlier.

Queen quietly savoured the thoughts of their earlier intimate indulgence once again. *Perhaps he is not as toned as most men his age, but the attraction is more than skin-deep.* She smiled softly, *besides he is as generous in the 'bedroom' as he is in general life.*

For a while they sat quietly staring into each other's eyes, sipping on their ruby-red Port. Mathew softly caressed Queen's legs which she draped sensuously over his lap.

She enjoyed the sweet sincerity of the moment, realising this had the potential for something more. They discussed the myriad of stars above, the echoing sounds of the wild, and even the early start for the hot air balloon trip the following morning.

Then out of the blue, it came.

"Queen, I've meant to inquire what you do for work?" He asked curiously, hoping the answer would not be what had been plaguing his mind the last few days.

Allowing her a moment to collect her thoughts, Queen took another slow sip, *Oh, I was hoping this moment would never come.* She leant forward to place the half-full glass on the table, as she considered whether to play 'the honest, yet confident' angle, or the deceptive half-truth.

Believing Mathew deserved honesty, she went with the former.

"Well, Mathew it is not so much a job than it is a lifestyle, I guess ..." she finally responded softly. He looked quizzically at her, as she continued, "I guess you could say some powerful men in my life reward me generously for my friendship."

A furrowed frown appeared on Mathew's forehead, and the caressing ceased. "Friendship? Could you maybe explain to me to what depth this 'friendship' actually extends?" He appeared full of questions now.

Feeling his eyes fixed on her, Queen was quiet at first. She realised this might be quite daunting for Mathew considering the level of vulnerability they experienced a little more than an hour ago. Then she began to explain.

"Mathew, this lifestyle is not something I predicted for my life, but ..."

Staring into the glowing fire rather than at her, Mathew broke her mid-sentence, "Are you intimate with these 'friends' Queen? How many 'friends' are there? Is Kgabu one of these so-called 'friends'?" His pitch began to rise.

Queen could see him slipping away from her making her even more reluctant to answer him now. She searched for the right words.

"Believe me, I never chose this, but it is what became of my life. It is all I now know Mathew, it provides me with a good life." Queen could feel herself building up her defensive wall, brick by brick.

"Look I had my suspicions when I saw you with Kgabu but chose to believe he was more of a mentor to you." Moving Queen's legs from his lap, Mathew hunched forward with his shaking head in his hands, "Geez Queen, I can't believe I was in such denial!"

Queen placed her hand on his back, "Mathew what I feel for you is different! Things won't always be this way for me, but I can't leave now. If you are willing to accept my lifestyle for what it is, to still be with me, then perhaps we can see what life holds for us in the future."

He looked at her puzzled and somewhat offended. "I'm not sure I can do that Queen. I have a reputation to uphold. I think you need to decide whether you want to be with me. Either you are in, or you are out!" He stated unequivocally.

They discussed the situation well into the night, with Mathew feeling deceived through his ignorant denial, and Queen defending a lifestyle she never wished for but in which she was now ensnared. She knew the doorkeeper would never let her out, not now, and certainly not for another man. Isaac would only let her go when his 'blessing' of her no longer suited him. Of course, the luxurious lifestyle that she currently enjoyed would then be ripped from her grasp.

Queen eventually rose from the couch. "Well, I'm exhausted and heading to bed. Perhaps your three months in Ghana will serve to provide us with both with the clarity we need."

"I think I will take the couch." He replied.

That night neither was able to find much sleep.

Having cancelled the balloon trip for an earlier than expected departure, they arrived back at the private airport. There was Khaya ready to fetch them, standing next to the car beaming his happy open smile. Surprised to receive a call to fetch them so early. Oblivious to the current circumstance, he happily welcomed them back but encountered a troubled couple who barely greeted him in return.

Queen was the first to be delivered to her building. Mathew exited the car to walk her inside. Khaya watched them exchanging some words before hugging each other goodbye.

Returning to his car, Mathew sat in the front passenger seat. Lost in deep contemplation. Khaya steered the car in silence, until Mathew finally spoke in a firm voice.

"Tomorrow, I am in and out of last-minute meetings all day. Would you mind using your car to fetch Queen at four-thirty and bring her to my home?"

"Sure, no problem Matt!" Khaya responded jovially, pretending he did not notice the heaviness in the air.

CHAPTER TWELVE

The 56-year-old politician was visiting his hometown of Durban. For many years, even before Mbali's arrival, Isaac had frequented Mthunzi's Tavern and VIP Lounge as an esteemed patron. Of course, as a most valued VIP guest, he enjoyed access to endless glasses of blue-labelled whiskey, of which he was rather fond. When sufficiently well-oiled, Isaac boasted of his political acquaintances and pending cabinet selection to all that cared to listen.

Subsequently, Mr Mthunzi would bow and scrape to Isaac knowing that being politically connected, the Tavern may be overlooked for many illicit crimes, such as having an expired alcohol licence, prostitution, money laundering and even drugs. Granted, it was a mutually beneficial relationship which Isaac made sure to capitalise on.

Isaac had married his childhood sweetheart, but as his popularity grew and he gained more of the limelight, his submissive wife withdrew further into the shadow. They had three children, and she was quite content to play the doting mother, accepting Isaac's desire to live the high life which included occasional escorts to affairs of state. Besides if she verbalised her discontent, Isaac might have beaten some 'sense' into her, as he was inclined to do. The violent threats crept into their marriage during the early stages, and she quickly learnt it was better to hold her tongue.

The power of his success and the copious intake of alcohol over the years had transitioned Isaac into a man of excessive arrogance, controlling and quick to temper. Upon their first meeting, Mbali was making her rounds at the VIP Lounge, filling empty glasses and collecting betting slips. Having endured the routine for almost a year and a half, she reluctantly yielded to Baba Mthunzi. A miserable life of captivity had reduced her once bright internal flame to just smouldering coals. Yet an occasional flicker, although dim, still held the promise of fire deep within her soul.

Just then Zanele made her way over to Mbali who stood waiting for Vusi at the bar. "The giant toad over there in the corner wants you. Careful!" Zanele indicated the direction with the motion of her head. When the two naïve Mthethwa girls first found themselves in this miserable underworld, Zanele had taken them under her wings as best she could. She was Mbali's confidant and closest friend, perhaps even like a sister as she had once promised.

Looking towards the corner of the room, Mbali saw Isaac beckoning her towards him. A cigar in one hand and a whiskey held tightly in the other. *Oh my goodness! Zanele is right! He does look like a content toad sitting on a giant green lily pad,* she thought as she tried not to laugh at the sight before her.

Mbali made her way towards him with her tray in hand. Isaac patted the jungle-green couch next to him. Mbali placed her small tray on the glass table and unenthusiastically sat beside Isaac. Previously warned of his erratic character, she felt even more exposed than usual. It was this innocent vulnerability that seduced Isaac.

"So, your name is Mbali I'm told," he slurred.

"Yes, it is Mr Mopantokobogo."

His chubby hand patted her leg as his eyes rested on the curves of her youthful cleavage. "Please … call me Isaac."

Trying not to flinch, Mbali nodded.

Isaac took a large gulp of whiskey causing some to dribble from the corner of his mouth. "How long have you worked here then Mbali?" He inquired.

The days had become so muddled to Mbali. They had worked days and nights in a dimly lit bar only retreating to the establishment's rooms at odd hours. Time was such a blur. She took a while to collect her thoughts. "It's been almost 20 months Mr Mo …. Isaac." Looking up, Mbali saw Zanele standing at the chrome balustrade nearby. She appeared to be listening.

"20 months you say. Hmmm, and how old would you be then?" Isaac questioned her further as his spongy fingers stroked her inner thigh just above her knee.

Mbali noticed Zanele attempting to disguise a shaking head with enlarged eyes but did not understand the cause for it. "I turn 18 in two weeks," Mbali replied and then promptly added, "And then I will be allowed out of the establishment for the first time."

"Ahhhh I see, so that means Mbali will be receiving a great gift in two weeks then," Isaac seemed to gleam with joy. "I will make sure I am here to help you celebrate." He tightened his grip around her thigh squeezing until it pained her.

"Ouch that hurts," she said looking at him quizzically.

Just then Zanele approached.

"My apologies Mr Mopantokobogo, but Mbali is needed by Mr Mthunzi now." Zanele swiftly escorted Mbali away by her elbow.

"Mbali! Why did you tell him that you are turning 18? Why!" Zanele exclaimed. "Anybody ... BUT him!"

"I don't understand Zanele, what is the big deal?" Mbali asked.

Zanele sighed. "Oh my darling Mbali, the celebration of your birthday is more for these filthy animals than it is for you! They call it a 'gift', but they take far more from you."

Looking around to make sure that no one was watching, Zanele took Mbali by the hand and led her to the staff smoking courtyard for privacy.

"Mbali the celebration of turning 18 at Mthunzi's Tavern is not a cause of celebration for us! It is a sordid night. You must show yourself to these men - Naked! Those that are interested in you will put money in envelopes to buy your time for the evening. These envelopes are part of the 'gift', and it is as if you should be grateful for it. Baba Mthunzi takes most of the money."

Zanele had not finished before Mbali interrupted, "But I don't care about the money! What matters most is that I get to leave this place! This is my chance!"

"Mbali! Listen you get to leave the Tavern, yes! But not alone! The man who puts the most money in the envelope can do what he likes to you, and you will not be out of his sight, or Tau's for that matter."

"But nothing bad will happen, right? Tau is our caretaker here!" Mbali responded.

Zanele shook her head, "Don't be stupid Mbali! First and foremost, Tau is on the payroll of Baba Mthunzi, and you are Baba's possession. Do you understand?"

At that moment, Mbali looked bewildered, like a small deer trapped in a snare. *Was this to be her Ayize moment?*

Zanele pulled Mbali close and held her tightly. Just then Tau popped his head through the door, "What's going on here? Get back to work!"

Zanele pushed passed Tau.

"Give her a damn break!" She snapped. "It's that time of the month, and she is missing her family."

CHAPTER THIRTEEN

Four-thirty on the dot, Khaya arrived to collect Queen, outside what many would consider a 'posh' high-rise residence. Mr Slade recognised Khaya before he stepped out from the medium-sized blue hatchback. He appeared surprised that such a regular-looking car would arrive for *Miss Queen*. Pressing the buzzer for Queen's apartment, Mr Slade relayed the message that her driver was here, before turning to Khaya.

"Miss Queen will just be a minute." Mr Slade relayed.

Distracted with moving items from inside the car to the boot, Khaya was startled when Queen suddenly appeared standing next to him, with her overnight bag in hand. "Afternoon Khaya," she chirped cheerfully.

Khaya jumped with surprise. "Gosh, you're in stealth mode today Queen?" Reaching for her bag, his hand touched hers. They paused for a moment, both felt the spark of electricity, but she quickly released her grip on the bag.

"Oh, so it's just 'Queen' today is it?" She questioned him teasingly, noticing the car boot littered with an array of books.

"I'm afraid so, I wasn't given specific instructions this time, but since you are in my car today, you might as well enjoy the usual overly confident, cheeky, yet oh-so-very-charismatic me!" He jested as he confidently strutted around to open the passenger door.

Queen let out a laugh. "Oh, my goodness! Refreshingly honest too I see! Well, that suits me just fine." She replied somewhat flirtatiously before lowering herself into the front passenger seat.

As Khaya sat behind the steering wheel, Queen asked, "excuse me for being so nosy, but what were all those books in the boot of your car?"

Khaya smiled, "Well actually I'm busy studying, and since I never know whether I will be studying at home, at work or soon at Matt's place while he is away, I tend to carry them with me."

"So, this is not your full-time job? Do you drive for Mathew during the holidays?" She quickly responded, beginning to place the puzzle pieces regarding the dynamics of the Mathew-Khaya relationship.

Khaya looked surprised, "wow you are a step ahead of me, you must be good at chess!" He declared, before waffling on with the specifics.

"My Dad instilled a strong work ethic in me, reminding me that his father was never so lucky to have opportunities in life. So even though there are university holidays, there are no 'real' holidays for me. Not if I wish to succeed in life!"

"I think that sounds a little harsh," Queen replied. "Everyone deserves a break now and again! Besides, you need time for your friends, and your girlfriend, surely?" She hoped this attempt to find out if he had a girlfriend was subtle enough.

Khaya instantly looked at Queen and grinned cheekily. "So, you want to know if I have a girlfriend, do you?" He teased her assertively.

Queen looked out the window and bit her lip to prevent herself from laughing at the situation in which she found herself. *Damn! Clearly, I wasn't subtle enough!* She said to herself.

"Well, firstly I have plenty of friends which I spend time with, and secondly, I don't have a girlfriend!" Khaya stated.

Queen smiled quite bashfully.

"Besides working with Matt can hardly be considered as work! I first met Matt when I was about eleven, then when I was fifteen, he needed people to hand out pamphlets on weekends. Of course, I was keen to earn some money during the holidays. My Dad said I could do it and it just snowballed from then." Khaya rambled on, "It's more like a fun introduction to the corporate world with a friend!" He was smiling that wondrous smile again, as he glanced over at Queen.

Queen admired him, and quietly considered his take on life, *here is a young man about my age, with the passion for making something of himself.* Juxtapositioning her life against his, she wondered, *Could I ever be with someone my age in this life?* Her thoughts spiralled quickly downwards. *Maybe, it's just karma for entering this lifestyle, and I am destined to be used and eventually thrown away?* Saddened by her internal dialogue she harshly reprimanded herself, *Oh, snap out of it Queen! Could you be any more melodramatic!*

Before she could ask what Khaya was studying, he asked her to click the grey button on the remote which was in the cubby. With that, the modern gate of the cluster housing complex began to slide open with a lazy groan.

"Well, here we are! Suburban bliss!" Khaya announced turning in to park in front of the wooden garage doors. Mathew appeared at the front door to welcome Queen to his contemporary 'sustainably designed' home.

"Well, thanks for the enjoyable chat Khaya," Queen said as she made her way around to retrieve her bag, now not wanting to leave the conversation hanging.

"Yet again the pleasure was all mine Queen. You have a good evening!" Khaya wished her with a mischievous wink. With that Khaya watched the most beautiful woman disappear behind the large swing door.

After Mathew's special homemade dinner of slow-braised lamb shank accompanied with all the trimmings, complemented by polite light-hearted conversation, the two sat by the flickering fire to indulge in deep bowls of Italian gelato. Then the conversation turned more serious.

"Queen, I have given some consideration to what we discussed last night, and ..." The shrill sound of Queen's cell-phone began echoing from her handbag.

"I'm sorry! Let me just turn it off," she said apologetically. Lifting the cell-phone from the side pocket of her handbag, she noticed the unmistakable initials "I.M." on the LED display. Queen chose to hide the identity of her 'gentlemen' by using only their initials. Her blood turned cold instantly! If she did not take the call, the results could be catastrophic for her. She looked at Mathew and noticed his intense stare waiting for her reaction. Considering the current conditions, Queen decided to turn the phone to 'silent' and return to the couch. Her heart was thumping out of her chest. She knew better than to trifle with Isaac Mopantokobogo. Panic seeped into every fibre of her body but she tried her best to hide it.

"As I was saying, I have given it some serious thought, and I may have a solution." Mathew watched as Queen settled back on the couch before he continued. "When I get back from my trip, why don't you come to live here with me, and let me provide for you?"

Queen never expected to hear such a suggestion, and now with the gentle reminder on her cell-phone, she was even less likely to consider this her route out.

"Mathew, I appreciate your offer, but how would that be any different to where I am now? There would still be a man providing for me, and I will feel trapped." She tried to explain in exact words without sounding ungrateful.

"Then I will organise a suitable position for you at the media company here? If it makes you feel better, you could start as an intern while I am away." Mathew searched for a workable solution, but all Queen could think about was the reaction of Isaac.

"Mathew, do you think that is wise?" She cocked a brow looking up to his gaze. "Kgabu owns the media company and I respect him too much to move in with his friend. Never mind seeking employment at one of his companies without him asking me himself." Queen responded in a matter-of-fact manner. "Think of the repercussions of what you are suggesting."

Mathew showed signs of frustration but attempted to remain calm. "Well, I'm not sure what to do Queen. I cannot accept things the way they are! Come to think of it, I even have trouble imagining it as part of your past, but I'm willing to try."

There was a prolonged silence. "Mathew, what happens if I give up all I have. I come here to live with you, and even intern, and you cannot look beyond my chequered history?" She questioned him firmly, without raising her voice, knowing he really did not know as much as he should about her.

No answer was forthcoming from Mathew. He was stumped.

Then Queen offered some sage advice. "Mathew, look I like you. I like you a lot and perhaps under different circumstances, we may have stood a chance, but the time is just not right for me now. Perhaps your time in Ghana is just at the right time for us both to consider what sacrifices and changes we could make."

"I guess you are right Queen. Perhaps, for now, we should leave it for what it is. Three months should give us time to reflect on how much of ourselves we are willing to bend, if at all." Mathew sounded concerned, yet sensible, as he collected the empty ice-cream bowls to take to the kitchen.

"I think we should call it a night," Mathew said as he picked up Queen's overnight bag, "If you would like to follow me, I've had the guest room made up for you. I think you will rest easy there."

And so, the evening concluded. Again, sleeping separately.

The Blessing of Queen

The smell of coffee brewing woke Queen from a deep slumber. She had thoroughly enjoyed her sleep, in fact, she awakened in the same position she remembered falling asleep. Muted voices filtered through the spacious house, one of which was a woman. Queen looked at the bedside clock. The bright green digits showed 10:10am.

ALREADY! Queen threw the duvet back and leapt from the bed. Without showering, she quickly dressed and made her way down to the modern sun-drenched kitchen. She found Mathew sitting alone at the dining table reading the Saturday paper. He looked up as she entered.

"Ahhh good morning Queen! I trust you slept well. Would you like Amelia to prepare her worldly breakfast for you?" He asked glancing towards the chubby middle-aged lady who was clearing away his dishes.

"Good morning Mathew. My apologies for sleeping in so late!" Queen felt somewhat awkward having company under these circumstances.

Queen smiled at Amelia who was waiting for her instruction.

"Good morning Amelia, I'm afraid I am not much of a breakfast person. So just a cup of coffee with milk, no sugar would be perfect for me. Thank you."

"Well, I have quite a few loose ends I have to tie up today. I do not mean to rush you Queen, but as soon as you are ready, I will drive you back to your place. If that's ok?" Mathew asked in an impassive tone.

Very little was said on the melancholic drive to Queen's apartment block, apart from the polite conversation regarding Mathew's initial plans for the Ghanaian market.

Veering from the freeway and turning towards Rosebank, a plane could be seen streaking across the sky, leaving a trail of cloud in its wake.

"I know this situation is somewhat precarious Queen, but would you at least consider coming with us to the airport tomorrow, even if just to say goodbye?"

Queen nodded in agreement, giving Mathew a quick smile.

"Great!" He smiled before continuing, "and one last thing - please use this time apart to reflect and consider all I have already suggested. You might find it makes sense."

"I will do that," Queen replied, suddenly distracted by the recollection of last night's missed call from Isaac. She needed to call him the moment she was alone and she had better have a believable reason for not answering his call.

CHAPTER FOURTEEN

Mbali woke to the sounds of whispers and muffled giggles. At first, she opened just one eye. She saw the girls standing around her bed. She quickly opened both eyes and sat up in a sleepy daze to see what was happening. Suddenly, the familiar song of "Happy Birthday" echoed through the room. The cheerful faces of the familiar girls danced and clapped merrily around her. Mbali rubbed her eyes. Unable to contain her laughter, she lay back on her elbow to appreciate the early morning exuberance.

At the foot of the bed stood Zanele holding a cake with 18 flickering candles punctured into the scarlet-coloured icing. Bold letters spelling "MBALI" emblazoned in lime green and white. The singing soon came to an end.

"Oh, and there is one more thing!" Zanele exclaimed and she encouraged Ayize to step from the back, holding not just one but two bottles of cheap champagne. "The cake is from us girls, and the bottles of fizz are from Baba," Zanele announced proudly.

At that moment in time, Mbali was the happiest she had been in a long while. These girls were her family now. Together they had saved to buy her this cake to make her day feel extra special.

Ayize was even partaking in the event, as she came forward to put the bottles on the nightstand. Mbali watched her intently hoping to see a glint of her sister in her eyes, but there was nothing. A stranger in her sister's body.

Now fully awake, Mbali hopped out of bed and took Ayize by the wrist before she could slouch away. Putting her arms around Ayize, Mbali held her longer and closer than ever, feeling how her body was becoming so gaunt and lifeless.

"Ayize, my big sister, I will always love you," Mbali whispered, but the response was merely a solemn nod as Ayize tried to twist free from the awkward embrace.

The girls all made their way to the living area, to enjoy cake and mugs of cheap champagne for breakfast. Hearing the early morning ruckus, even Tau came through to wish Mbali, reminding her that this was an important day for her. Mbali secretly hoped that being her birthday she would be excluded from working today, but it was Friday and so a busy night for the VIP Girls. Besides, the worst part is what Zanele had told her two weeks before, although Mbali still did not comprehend how different this night would be for her.

The shift started the same as every other. It was all routine now for Mbali: walk down the dimly lit stairs; the Tavern girls in front; the VIP girls in their 'little black numbers' at the rear; each let in on Tau's command.

Tonight, however, the VIP Lounge seemed busier than usual, Mbali squeezed herself through the crowd to greet her regular admirers. She wondered if Baba had put the word out, or how else would all these people know to wish her. Apart from the unusually lustful greetings, the night appeared to go ahead as usual.

Then around 9:15pm, Mbali was summoned to Baba's office. She scuttled behind Tau realising this was the first time she had been there since arriving. The only sound was that of her heels clicking on the tiled floor as they tottered towards the heavy wooden door. She entered to find Baba lounging in his executive chair behind a bulky and cluttered wooden desk. His feet rested on the desk, crossed at the ankles. The typical cloud of cigar smoke hung heavily around him. To the right was Patricia lounging comfortably on the well-worn leather couch.

"Welcome my Little Princess," he cooed at Mbali, "and a happy birthday to you! Come here so I can congratulate you."

Mbali made her way behind the desk allowing Baba to give her a hug and a slobbery peck on the cheek before he gestured for her to take a seat.

"Tonight is a big night for you Mbali! Not only do you celebrate turning 18, but your customers would like to bestow some gifts on you. The one with the most generous gift will allow you to leave the Tavern! Isn't that exciting?" Baba sounded most enthused.

Apprehensive and afraid of what this night might unveil, Mbali softly acknowledged him. "Yes Baba." The memory of Isaac's smirk as he inflicted pain on her two weeks earlier flashed across her mind. Thankfully, she had not seen him in the lounge tonight which, at least, lay some of her anxiety to rest.

"To receive these gifts, there is a bit of a ritual here at the VIP Lounge." Baba stared intently at Mbali. "I have asked Patricia to explain it all, and to dress you appropriately."

He turned his head in the direction of Patricia. "Patricia make sure she is back in the lounge at 10:00pm!"

Baba took a deep breath and rocked his body twice to gain the momentum to propel himself from the eternally groaning chair. He lumbered with a wheezing breath, out of the room.

It was now 10:00pm.

There Mbali stood.

Alone.

Clothed in a gold satin robe, yet barefoot on the familiar plush red carpet of the VIP Lounge. The only difference is the thick red velvet curtains that were usually drawn open, were now closed to conceal the VIP Lounge from the Tavern below. The other VIP girls vacated, leaving only the VIP guests standing in a semi-circle, many clutching sealed white envelopes.

Baba Mthunzi entered the room and stood next to Mbali.

"Good evening esteemed patrons of Mthunzi's VIP Lounge," he announced optimistically. "Tonight, we have a great celebration! Our lovely Mbali is now 18 and ready to receive her generous gifts."

Gesturing with the slow sway of his hand, he presented Mbali. The row of contented men, eagerly raised their clunking glasses to her in agreement, "Cheers to Mbali!" They roared liked hungry hyenas dressed in business suits.

Mbali froze. Although she recognised many of these faces, the circumstance felt completely foreign to her. Baba gave her a light nudge of encouragement, "Go ahead, Little Princess..."

Had it not been for the shots of tequila that Patricia insisted she drink, Mbali would have run frantically from the room. With the edges of reality blurred, slowly Mbali began to unfold the satin band around her waist, she clenched her teeth as the golden robe slipped silently to her feet. There she stood in all naked vulnerability, just like the day she was born. The men looked at her in admiration, some smirked, some nudged, some whispered, but all were in awe of her youthful perfection.

As instructed by Patricia earlier, Mbali bent over to retrieve the small woven basket from the glass table. Then starting from the right-hand-side she began accepting the generous enveloped offerings.

Each envelope placed in the trembling basket was exchanged for a humiliated murmur: "Thank you for your gift."

Mbali avoided making eye contact as she worked her way down the line. Reaching the end of the row of glaring, watching, staring eyes she returned to her spot, marked only by the golden gown lying in a shiny heap on the floor.

Just as Mbali attempted to pick up the protection of the gown, a deep voice bellowed from behind the row of standing gawkers.

"What about my envelope?"

The familiar voice sent shivers down Mbali's bare spine. It was Isaac M! He did not even bother to shift from his usual couch, for he knew from two weeks back of his interest.

As pathway cleared amongst the hyenas, Mbali apprehensively made her way through the row of leering eyes, skimming every part of her exposed flesh. On the verge of tears, Mbali felt dirty and ashamed. She attempted to hide her most intimate area with the woven basket.

Isaac grinned self-importantly as he dropped his envelope into the basket. With a subtle moan of gratification, his eyes wandered longingly over her nakedness. He took a large swig of amber whiskey.

"Thank you for your gift," Mbali replied with her head down to hide the tears that had collected in her despairing eyes.

She returned once more to the golden heap on the floor. Tau was standing there to collect the now full basket. He swiftly strode out the VIP lounge behind Baba to inspect the envelopes in the privacy of the office. Mbali was left alone, clambering to cover her dignity once more. The men quenched their dry mouths with the remnants of alcohol in their glasses. The air was thick with the anticipation of the pending results.

The other VIP Girls entered the lounge each looking to see how Mbali was coping with the situation. Instead of showing compassion, they mingled the men to capitalise on their high spirits.

Zanele hurried over to Mbali and took her hand. She squeezed it tight. "Mbali, go quickly to Patricia! Ask her to give you something special for tomorrow before you leave! She will know what you mean." With that Mbali left to change back into her working clothes and find Patricia.

As promised, it was Isaac who had generously outbid his opponents, not so much with money, but rather with the promise to overlook the establishment's misdeeds for yet another year. Such an undisclosed commitment from a politician as powerful as Isaac was worth much more to Baba than cash. To give the process authenticity, Isaac supplied a sealed envelope, but unlike all the others which of contained money his was empty.

Baba Mthunzi gave his *Little Princess* a final pep-talk as she tried to discreetly dress her quivering body in his office.

"You be good to Isaac, you hear? He has offered you a great gift. A rite of passage to become a real woman. You should be grateful to be chosen by such a powerful man."

Tau and Baba proceeded to vigorously tear open each envelope, dividing the money into two piles. Two-thirds for Baba and one-third for Mbali. Placing Mbali's pile of dirty banknotes into an envelope, Baba handed it to her.

"You see how generous your customers are!"

Then he and Tau left to announce the 'good' news to the men crowing loudly at one another in the lounge.

For Mbali, what had so far turned into an awful night, was about to get even worse. Isaac's chauffeur-driven car with tinted windows pulled from the Tavern grounds. Soon they were speeding along the freeway towards the sparkling city lights of Durban. Isaac heaved himself across the seat closer to Mbali. She sat immobilised on the cold black leather. His drunken hand reached up between her legs forcing her legs apart.

"No!" She yelped in a high pitch, "Please don't!"

He laughed at her as she tried to push his plump hand away. "You can fight as much as you like, but we have ALL night Mbali!"

He tried again, more forcefully. This time Mbali just switched her mind off. She watched the twinkling lights that reflected off the puddles of rain that had fallen earlier in the evening. Imagining herself somewhere else. Somewhere safe. Distracted, she realised that Isaac was squeezing her hand against his engorged erection. She felt repulsed. Mbali moved her face with teeth clenched, just as he tried to kiss her with his drooling mouth, rank with the concoction of fried food, whiskey, and cigars.

The car entered a dimly lit parking area and headed for a line of trees. The chauffeur parked the car and then took his leave. The bright lights of another vehicle parking nearby gave Mbali a glimmer of hope that someone else was nearby. She pulled on the shiny silver door handle hoping to escape but soon learnt the wrath of Isaac's heavy-handedness. Hands that he gladly used to subdue the countless 'insolent and untamed' women many times before. Women such as young Mbali Mthethwa.

He forced Mbali to use her mouth to satisfy him for the first time that night, right there in the dimly-lit parking lot of a luxury hotel. Satisfied, he zipped his pants closed, then knocked on the car window with his chunky gold signet ring for the driver to open the door.

Mbali stepped out. Timid and fractured.

Her usually big shiny doe-eyes, tinged with red from salty tears. Her sweet and innocent face now distraught and fearful. She peered over to the other car, hoping for someone willing to help her, but only saw Tau leaning against the driver's door. He merely nodded at her, indicating that he was watching her. Isaac took Mbali firmly by the arm, ushering her towards the private entrance of the villa. Tau trailed a short distance behind.

The darkest night of Mbali's life also seemed to be the longest. Beaten into submission she finally accepted Isaac's chosen method of violation. He continually reminded her of the rite of passage he was bestowing on her. The gift of becoming a woman, as he held her down with the weight of his body. There were flashes of moments when Isaac was inside her that Mbali began to understand why Ayize turned to drugs. The perpetual 'high' must have provided relief from the reality of enduring such nightly violations.

Mimicking the actions of Ayize which Mbali had witnessed from Lounge above, she made a point of taking swigs of whichever alcohol was within hands reach between the bouts of bullying. It became apparent to Mbali that she was a means to fulfil Isaac's insatiable and vile desires. His demeaning commands were designed merely to break her determined spirit. Mbali eventually succumbed, believing indifference would be her sole means of survival.

When the day finally broke, Isaac was asleep and snoring loudly. Mbali quietly picked her battered and bruised body up from the bed. She stumbled towards the bathroom to relieve herself. Slipping her black dress over her throbbing bruised shoulders, she slowly sat on the toilet. On relieving herself she immediately winced when she felt a stinging sensation that quickly morphed into one of excruciating pain, it felt like she was torn.

Standing to clean her tear-stained face at the marble basin, Mbali did not expect the appalling sight that stared back at her through swollen eyes. She moved her gaze from that unrecognisable blank face, tenderly touching her aching lips stained with dry blood. She wondered: *what have I done to deserve this life?*

Remembering the pill that Patricia told her to take "immediately" the next morning, Mbali tiptoed back to the bedroom to get her handbag. Returning to the bathroom she tried to clean herself up as best she could, with the little makeup she had brought with her. Mbali noticed the envelope Baba gave her the night before with the cash inside. "It looks like at least R5,000!" She exclaimed quietly.

Suddenly Mbali had an idea. *Perhaps no one is outside the door now!* Her mind kicked into gear. *This money can help me escape these animals! I can run to a place where no one can find me! I can go home!*

Isaac was still snoring. Mbali gathered her belongings back into her handbag. She quietly tiptoed through the bedroom into the living room. She picked up her scuffed stilettos in the passage and made her way to the front door. With her hand on the brass doorknob, Mbali held her breath as she slowly twisted her wrist until the door latch was free.

She looked back to make sure Isaac was not creeping up behind her, then slowly pulled the door ever so quietly towards herself.

It opened.

She peeped through the crack.

The coast looks clear! Her heart was beating like thunder.

She opened the door further popping her head out to check the entire corridor. There was a chair against the wall, but no driver and no Tau.

Taking a deep breath, Mbali took one step forwards into freedom. There was a short corridor, and then the outside world. Struggling to breathe from the trepidation surging through her body, Mbali closed the door just so it was left ajar in case she needed to get back in. She walked swiftly but softly towards the double glass doors, sensing the opportunity of escape finally within her grasp.

As she rounded the corner, there Tau stood leaning against the outside balustrade facing her with a cigarette in his hand. Mbali stopped dead in her tracks nothing but a sheet of glass separated them. Tau looked directly at her through the glass doors, before walking towards her.

"What are you doing Mbali?" he growled at her, "You think you can escape, do you?" He said grabbing her wrist tightly.

Mbali could not believe she came so near to freedom.

"No! No Tau! You have it all wrong!" Attempting to sound as sincere as possible. She needed to think quickly!

"Then why are you here?" He demanded angrily, shaking her arm tightly as he walked her back towards the room.

"I'm ... I'm just hungry after last night Tau! I wanted to thank Isaac for the gift of becoming a woman." Mbali felt an urge to throw-up, but continued. "He must be hungry this morning, so I was going to buy breakfast! I was ... Umm ... I was looking for someone to help me so I can order, as I didn't want to wake him using the phone." Mbali sounded truly believable, as she showed Tau the money.

Growing up with her mischievous siblings, Mbali had discovered her talent of always having an answer for everything, but one thing her work at the VIP Lounge taught her, was how good she was at weaving fabricated lies into believable words.

Tau looked directly at her attempting to read her intentions, then considered perhaps some truth lay in this as she could have just phoned for help, or even tried to buy her way past him, which she did not.

"Alright, I'm going to take you back to the villa now, and I will organise room service for you." He promptly walked her back down the passage. "Don't worry. You will not need to pay for it. Mr Isaac has more than enough money."

Isaac was still snoring and wheezing for air when Mbali returned to sit quietly on the tub chair next to the window. Hugging her slender legs to her chest, she enjoyed the warmth of the morning sun kissing her tender skin. Her body felt less tense now that she had moved about to stretch the aching muscles. Using this moment of quiet, Mbali contemplated how she could make the best opportunity from this dire predicament.

Less than 40-minutes later the quietness in the villa was roused by the loud knocking at the front door. Although expecting the visit, Mbali still jumped with fright knowing that the noise might awaken the snoring, gasping beast lying in the bed.

Isaac woke, surprised by the commotion. He looked quizzically at Mbali as she stood up from the chair. "I just wanted to thank you for the gift, so I have ordered breakfast. I hope that it is to your liking." She walked from the room towards the door to the villa.

Isaac watched her leaving and was somewhat stunned by the reception he had just received. Such gratitude is not what he expected this morning, after all, he had been quite unrelenting with her. Isaac was both puzzled and intrigued by the strength of this young woman before him.

Mbali noted how Isaac's demeanour changed after she turned the tables and appeared to dote on him. He interacted with her in a far less crude manner. This morning Isaac did not attempt to touch Mbali. Not even once.

Mbali inconspicuously moved her breakfast around her plate, as she watched Isaac stuffing his face with everything within arm's reach. As the time neared 09:00am, Tau made his appearance to let them know that soon it was time for her to leave. Collecting her small handbag, Mbali thanked Isaac for allowing her to leave the Tavern for the night. As strange as it felt, she nervously leant down to Isaac who was still seated and gave him a Judas-hug with her bruised arms.

He looked at what he had done to her. "Wait here!" He ambled through to the bedroom again.

A feeling of dread filled Mbali, for she was indeed ready to leave his evil presence without any further delay.

Isaac returned, placing a folded wad of crispy notes into Mbali's palm, then with what sounded like a touch of remorse. "This is for you. Please buy yourself something nice for when I see you next."

Mbali closed her fingers over it and wanted to scream: "*Yes I will accept your guilt money!*" but instead she meekly replied, "Thank you, Isaac. I will do that." She left the upmarket villa to join Tau outside.

On the 25-minute drive back to Mthunzi's, Mbali's bruised little body sat motionless as she reflected on last night's experience. How vicious Isaac was at first, yet how mouldable he was when she took the initiative to 'reward' him. She recalled his look of surprise as if he had managed to tame her. *As if I would ever let him control my mind!* She thought angrily.

Mbali clutched her little bag in her hands feeling the thickness on account of the money it now held. She had genuinely believed that last night would afford her opportunity to escape. Watching the pedestrians pass by, Mbali quietly considered her next steps. *OK so my escape plan did not go as I expected, but if I continue to use my wiles to manipulate Isaac, perhaps I still have a chance.*

CHAPTER FIFTEEN

Mbali did not need to wait long, for it appeared Isaac could think of nothing other than her. He yearned to have her, to control her. Each of the following nights Isaac returned to the VIP lounge to bask in the splendour of the woman he believed he had created. To his dismay, Mbali was not working because the inflicted cuts and bruises required time to heal. Her absence spurred Isaac's desire to possess her, to grow even more intensely.

On Wednesday evening, Mbali finally entered the VIP Lounge. Isaac was sitting in his usual corner smoking a fat, earthy cigar, with an expensive whiskey in his hand. He immediately summoned Mbali over to him. She smiled and took a seat on his lap.

"Mbali, my dear, I will be returning to Johannesburg on Friday evening."

Not sure whether to be elated or to be concerned that her potential ticket out of Mthunzi's was slipping away, she responded with a phoney smile. "Oh, Mr Isaac I'm going to miss seeing you."

During her time working at the Tavern, Mbali honed the skill of escaping from her stark reality, while giving the men around her just enough to keep them paying for more of her time. The manipulation was far easier than she ever imagined. It required little more than a soft touch of a hand, a breathy whisper in the ear, or the stoking of their massive egos before making her attendance scarce by giving her affections to another.

Isaac was thrilled to hear of her missing him. "I too will miss our special friendship Mbali, especially since I don't know when work will bring me back to this area again." He replied in his usual slurry baritone voice. He stroked her thigh in circular motions, moving ever higher.

Trying not to cringe, Mbali faked a gloomy pout. She sat delicately on his lap with her big doe-eyes looking directly at him while she toyed with his loosened tie. "Perhaps Mr Isaac can take me with?" She cooed teasingly as his brain contemplated his options.

After a few moments, Isaac's hand moved from the hollow of her back down to her rounded buttocks, where he patted her lightly before giving them a firm squeeze. "Be a good girl Mbali and let Baba know I wish to talk business with him." Mbali smiled knowingly.

It was a sunny Friday afternoon when Mbali was called once again to Baba's smoke-filled office. She knocked on the door lightly. Tau opened the door abruptly. Upon entering the dingy room, Mbali saw Isaac reclining on the well-worn leather couch and Baba in his usual relaxed position.

"Ah come in Little Princess," Baba crooned from behind his large wooden desk.

With a feeling of apprehension, Mbali walked gradually to the middle of the room. With each step, she felt the filthy glare of eyes upon her once more.

"Mr Isaac has expressed interest in you joining him in Johannesburg. I would like to know what your thoughts are?"

Mbali realised this was her opportunity to change her life, to finally leave this place and make life better for herself. She knew that she would need to tread most carefully with her words now so as not to offend either of them.

She looked at Baba Mthunzi first. "Baba, you are always going to be my only Baba, and I will always be your Little Princess." Mbali fought the reflex to frown in anger as speaking these words.

"... but Mr Isaac has shown me how to be a real woman. He is the only man I have been with, and he has indeed given me a gift, for which I will always be grateful." Mbali forced these vile words from her lips almost convincing herself.

Pausing momentarily, she looked over to Isaac.

"If Mr Isaac wishes to have me with him, then I would be glad to offer him that." An intense feeling of illness crept into Mbali's stomach, and she tried to keep from heaving.

The Blessing of Queen

The two men looked at each other. Baba Mthunzi was the first to speak. "Isaac ... I accept your lucrative offer of affording my business dealings the protection I require. As for the generous amount discussed, this should be transferred to my private account before you take possession." Isaac stood, nodding his head as he leant forward to shake Baba's hand.

Possession? Really? It is like buying a pair of shoes. Mbali felt disgusted but elated at the same time. *I cannot wait to tell the girls that I am finally out of here!*

Isaac beckoned Mbali over with his arms open for a hug. Knowing the repercussions, she robotically stepped forward to provide him with a false embrace.

Baba was beaming with his lucrative trade. "My dear Mbali you might have been my Little Princess, but you are soon to graduate as a queen."

Isaac crowed in agreement, "Aha yes! So true my friend!" Then he looked at Mbali, "I think from now on I will call you Queen. I believe that it is most fitting."

Mbali did not need to think long, for she also agreed that Queen was indeed a strong and regal name. She whispered to herself, *Yes, the day I step through the doors of this hellhole I will be Queen.* She smiled softly, knowing she just achieved the first step in her grand plan.

"Right Mbali, you can leave us to discuss the details now." Baba nodded at Tau who opened the door for her to leave.

Two weeks later, the day came for Mbali to depart on her adventure beyond the walls of Mthunzi's. It was a bittersweet day indeed, for she would leave behind not only Zanele and the girls she adored, but also her sister Ayize who had grown even more removed from her. The tears flowed effortlessly as each was hugged goodbye - some just a little tighter than others. Mbali promised that one day she would return, which secretly neither the girls nor Mbali really believed, but it just seemed like the right thing to say.

Tau knocked on the door. "Mbali it's time to go to the airport now."

Mbali took one more look at all the sombre faces she loved.

"See you all soon my friends!" She blew them a dramatic kiss with both hands then turned and left the girl's quarters.

It was nearly two years since Mbali first entered the door of Mthunzi's Tavern as a naïve young girl of just 16. Now she was 18 and leaving as a woman having immense inner fortitude. For the first time since leaving the safety of Gogo's arms, Mbali felt in control of her own destiny.

Today she was leaving as "Queen".

CHAPTER SIXTEEN

Stepping from the plane in Johannesburg, Queen felt a little insecure not knowing the procedure. This was the first time she had flown so she chose to follow the person in front of her. Soon she was standing in the baggage area waiting to collect the fuchsia-coloured luggage bag that Isaac's money had bought her. The bag was only medium-sized, and even still it was only half-filled with her favourite items.

There was little that Queen wished to bring with her into her new life. Most of her possessions were given to Zanele and Ayize. What she did pack were a few personal grooming products and one change of clothes still with their tags. Most importantly she packed a small blue shoebox containing the crumpled banknotes she earned over the last two years and two photos. One of her beautiful mother and siblings standing with Gogo and the other was a group photo of the 'Mthunzi Girls'. It was this instant that she realised this was the second time she was leaving her family behind.

Exiting 'Domestic Arrivals' Queen's bewildered doe-eyes hid the loss of her innocence well. Dressed conservatively in blue jeans, a figure-hugging long-sleeved T-shirt covered by a faux fur waistcoat and a pair of knee-high boots. She searched the faces in the waiting crowd for familiarity. Then she saw him. Isaac Mopantokobogo, sitting with his attention fixated on his phone, instead of on the arrivals.

The thought crossed her mind to disappear into the bustling crowd, but instead, Queen walked up to her nemesis.

"Hello Isaac," she said confidently.

He looked up. "Good morning, glad your flight was on time."

Queen gave him a peck on his chubby cheek, noticing that apart from the spicy cologne he used, she could also smell stale coffee and a hint of garlic. *Ughhh! Probably last night's supper.*

"Look, I wanted to fetch you for the first time so that you had a familiar face, but I have limited time to spend with you this week." Isaac hurriedly started making his way to the parking area, as he continued talking, "I will quickly take you to your new lodgings. Once there I will explain our arrangement."

Queen followed hastily behind with her brightly coloured luggage, continuously nodding in agreement. She did not wish to inadvertently trigger his temper so prematurely, by being less than attentive.

"Wow!" Queen gasped as she entered the spacious and empty apartment on the top floor. "Is this all for me?" She asked Isaac in disbelief.

"Yes, it is for you to use, as long as we have this mutual arrangement in place."

Queen was in awe as she surveyed the spacious room. Holding her breath, she wandered quietly around the airy living room with a sliding door opening onto a balcony. There was an open plan kitchen with modern steel appliances, that flowed into the dining area; then down a passage to the bedroom with a magnificent en-suite bathroom and another small balcony overlooking the leafy suburb.

"You will notice that there is minimal furniture Queen," Isaac announced as he followed her through the empty rooms. "That is because I want you to furnish it in your preferred style. There is a bed with new linen for you, but everything else ... you must purchase."

Queen looked at him, "But Isaac I don't know how to ... and... and ...," she stuttered with her voice shaking.

He cut her off mid-sentence. "I have a computer guy coming here this afternoon to spend some time with you. He will bring you a laptop and will teach you how to work the building internet. That way you can order items such as food and anything else you need to have delivered for now." Isaac stated matter-of-factly.

Queen nodded regimentally.

"I will pay for anything and everything you will ever need Queen. Once you are settled you can learn to drive, so you can go out and do these things for yourself. There is just one thing I want from you in return."

Queen waited anxiously for what he expected for all this. "When I want your time, you must be available to me. I do not mind if you have other friends, but I am to be above all others. ALWAYS! Do you understand this?"

"Yes Isaac, you will be number one," she answered submissively.

"Good. I am glad you understand because you do not want to make me angry." He stared at her intently with eyes that appeared to darken to black.

Again, Queen nodded fearing to maintain eye contact for too long, in case he might mistake that for a challenge.

"Alright, I have to go now. Here is a mobile phone with my number already in it. Make sure you always keep this phone with you, Queen! And I mean ALWAYS!" He fixed his eyes firmly on hers again, before adding: "Now David will be here at midday with the laptop to spend the afternoon with you. I will check in with you later."

Having chosen to have the lifestyle of a 'blessed' woman, Queen needed to continually suppress any desire to be her former self. Occasionally, in the corners of her mind, Queen would catch a faint flicker of Mbali's lightness, but it was only in her private space and time that Queen allowed Mbali to surface.

Four days had passed since arriving in what Queen soon discovered was the area of Rosebank. Furniture and décor items arrived steadily throughout the week, and the apartment was beginning to take shape, as was her closet. Often Queen found herself admiring a newly purchased outfit in front of the gilded mirror.

My innocence may be conquered, but this is just the first step to me becoming a woman of substance, she reminded herself.

Every day Queen grew stronger and wiser, but she did not venture out of the building. She had gone as far as the front foyer, where she met an elderly gentleman named Mr Slade. Smartly dressed in his burgundy jacket, Mr Slade was the resident doorman with a most friendly disposition. During one of their many pleasant conversations, he explained the immediate surroundings to her. With this new knowledge, she would then attempt to identify the landmarks from her windows above. Leaving the building was not an option for Queen, at least not until Isaac agreed.

Tonight, she would ask him as he was coming by after work to take her for supper. For Queen, tonight was to be a momentous challenge. Usually, she was the one entertaining within the confines of her space at Mthunzi's, but now she would be in public. It was all foreign to her, and she felt the burden of being tested.

To ensure she began the evening well Queen bought Isaac his favourite, blue-labelled whiskey. After scouring countless fashion magazines during the week, Mbali noticed a photograph staged at a dinner table. Considering her social ineptness, she felt compelled to order the exact outfit, complete with the shoes and jewellery. It had all arrived perfectly on time, the day before.

Queen heard the front door close. Placing the hairbrush on the dressing table, she walked through to the living room. Isaac laid his keys on the entrance hall table, before removing his jacket. His white shirt showed large sweat stains at the armpits. He looked at Queen pleasingly.

"You have done well Queen, the apartment looks nice," he slurred making his way towards her.

Queen smiled. "Good evening Isaac it is so nice to see you. May I get you a whiskey while I finish dressing?" She asked as she kissed him unenthusiastically on his thick lips.

"Yes, I need one tonight. It has been a trying day," he muttered as he watched her walking towards the drinks cabinet in her silky silver gown.

He observed how the ethereal fabric skimmed her enticing curves as she walked towards him.

Queen carefully placed the tumbler glass on the table next to him. "Here you go, one whiskey straight up!" She said playfully just as she would have done at Mthunzi's.

Before she could leave, he grabbed her arm.

"And where do you think you are going?" He asked as he twisted her arm, forcing her to her knees. "I told you I had a trying day. Shouldn't you try to fix that first?" He sneered.

Since beginning work at Mthunzi's, Queen practised suppressing her immediate feelings each time a man groped or fondled her. More recently she had mentally prepared herself for the reality that such times with Isaac would be her biggest challenges to endure. Fortunately, the arrangement was that she would only see him once or twice a week. Like Ayize's mantra when they first worked at Mthunzi's, Queen reminded herself that this torture would be temporary.

"Of course, I would like nothing better than to improve your mood," Queen said twisting her wrist from his tight grip to unzip his work trousers. Isaac took a sip of whiskey and leaned back into the couch cushions. He watched her with his free hand placed firmly on the back of her head.

While Isaac uttered the disgusting sounds of his pleasure, Queen imagined a young Mbali with a glowing future, complete with a family of her own. Living in a modest home with a kind husband that adored her. A flowered garden with perhaps two children and even a little dog, just as she saw in magazines.

Two hours later, Isaac was watching Queen across the dinner table enjoying her prawn tagliatelle. The restaurant was alive with the infectious laughs of happy people enjoying each other's company. In comparison, Table # 8 was subdued, and surprisingly quiet. Feeling intimidated under these circumstances, Queen struggled to make conversation.

She is an alluring young woman, Isaac thought in silence, *but I am in charge of her. I have tamed her, and for that, she reaps the benefits.* He shovelled food into his greedy blubbery mouth, yet still managed to smirk. *I never imagined she would be so receptive.*

More than that, he was intrigued by the resilience she showed, when he was heavy-handed with her. *If she ever waivers on our agreement, I will destroy her. She will be left with nothing.* He smiled at his fortunate situation of having the means to possess this creature of exquisiteness.

Queen looked up from her meal. "Isaac, I wanted to ask you, if it is alright for me to leave the apartment to explore the area. Only if that is okay with you?" Queen asked timidly.

"That is fine Queen. You are not my prisoner. You are my chosen." For a moment, Isaac sounded almost sincere, but Mbali knew better than to consider it a free ticket. "Just remember to take your phone with you. I would like for you to arrange driving lessons too, I have my eyes on a particular car for you."

For the first time in Isaacs company, Queen smiled sincerely in disbelief. "Really!? Driving? My very own car? Wow! Isaac, I don't know what to say!" Her eyes were shining bright with possibility.

A few minutes later Queen was still smiling when she held his chubby hand across the table. She reasoned that perhaps the occasional act of hostility or unpleasant favour, was not all bad if this was the payoff. She quietly reconciled: *If I avoid making mistakes to cause his anger then I do not believe this will be too difficult. Besides the more challenging the work, the better the reward!*

"Queen, next week Saturday I have a charity auction to attend. My wife is not interested in these events, so you will join me." Isaac informed her between mouthfuls. "Besides, maybe you can bid on a piece of artwork for your walls. You should also buy something smart for the evening, perhaps something in red would appeal."

Esjay C. Moore

"That would be wonderful Isaac! I look forward to it, and you won't be disappointed!" Queen now appeared to sparkle as she spoke.

CHAPTER SEVENTEEN

The elevator made its usual droning clicking noise as it heaved its way upward. Queen reached into her large handbag to retrieve her phone from the side pocket. She had not looked at the phone since she turned it to silent during the pivotal conversation with Mathew last night.

"Oh No! Seven missed calls!" She muttered anxiously, "what on earth am I going to tell him?"

She needed to think fast because as she stepped from the elevator, the phone began ringing with "I.M." yet again. She answered immediately rambling an apology. "Hello Isaac! I'm so sorry! Please let me explain!" She begged the spaces between her words were shorter than they ought to have been.

"Explain then!" Isaac demanded abruptly.

Always being able to think quickly under duress Queen hesitantly spun her tale. "I walked to the shops yesterday afternoon, and I was trying on some clothes, and the phone must have fallen from my pocket! I looked everywhere for it last night and then I went to the store again this morning and thankfully, they had it! I am just arriving home now. I'm so very sorry, please forgive me!" She pleaded desperately.

The phone went dead. Isaac had ended the call. Queen did not know what to make of it. She took a deep breath and decided to take a hot shower in the hope that she would feel better afterwards. Selecting some upbeat 70's disco tracks to lighten her mood, Queen then stepped into the steaming cubicle.

With her wet hair freshly oiled and arranged in a towelling turban, she wrapped a fluffy beige towel around her svelte figure and walked through to get something cool to drink from the refrigerator. She peered into the cooling compartment. *Hmmm, I think something fruity is just what I need!* She grabbed the colourful carton from the open door, then turned to get a glass from the cupboard behind her. Before she could, someone seized her by the throat and slammed her up against the cold steel refrigerator, knocking the air from her lungs.

"Do you think I am playing with you, Queen?" Isaac bellowed at her. His face was so close to hers that she could smell his putrid breath. Dropping the carton to the floor Queen tried to lessen his python-like grip from around her throat.

It got even tighter.

"Do you think I am stupid?" He shouted. "I have a tracker on your phone I can see your phone was not in the neighbourhood all night! Do you think you can lie to me, after everything I have done for you?" The pressure on her throat was unbearable.

Queen could do nothing but gurgle while desperately grabbing at his hands. Then he punched her squarely in the stomach. Again! And Again! He threw her to the floor, while he continued to throw punches at her small, crumpled body.

Grabbing her hair, he slammed her head against the cabinet, until a trickle of blood fell.

"Let me remind you who you are dealing with!" He continued in a threatening tone, "I rescued you from that slum, Queen! I could destroy your life as fast as I blessed it! Do you get that?"

Lying curled in a foetal position Queen begged desperately. "I'm sorry Isaac! I won't do that again! I'm sorry!" She clutched at the excruciating pain in her side.

Standing hovering over her, he shouted down with such venom that Queen could feel the spit from his mouth falling on her raised forearm.

"I give you everything you need, everything! You owe me, so why do you treat me this way?" He was beginning to sound almost pathetic to Queen, as she began to gather her inner courage.

Queen raised herself onto her hands and knees, still holding her side. She glared at this beast before her. "Beating me is not going to change things. I told you I am sorry, and I won't do that again! What more do you want from me?" She spoke through bloodied lips.

"Are you getting clever with me Queen?" Isaac glared at her, and with that, he crashed her head sideways into the fridge, and suddenly all went black. Queen collapsed motionless in a heap on the cold kitchen floor.

Isaac stood over her for a moment. She lay there lifeless. Unconscious, but still breathing. He wiped the sweat from his furrowed brow, then turned and left as if nothing had happened.

The bouncy, happy sounds of the '70s echoed cheerily through the luxurious apartment.

A sometime later, Queen stirred from her unconscious state. Dazed and confused she agonisingly stumbled her way to the bedroom. Struggling to breathe, she called for an ambulance, before slipping back into the dark abyss.

Within what seemed to be minutes, the caretaker unlocked the apartment for the paramedics. The angels in red uniforms, carefully placed her on a gurney assisting her to breathe with an oxygen breathing apparatus. Soon a semi-conscious Queen was being wheeled through the front doors of the building. Mr Slade watched on with a concerned look on his furrowed face. It was nearly eight o'clock when Queen disappeared behind the doors of the ambulance destined for the hospital.

CHAPTER EIGHTEEN

Between packing his bags and making last-minute business calls, Mathew intended to phone Queen to let her know what time they would fetch her, but as usual, time was just getting away from him.

Having seen Khaya driving up the driveway, Mathew gathered his bags. He locked his front door whilst reminding himself to call Queen on the way. As he placed the heavy luggage into the car-boot, Mathew called over to Khaya.

"Good morning Khaya! Please remember to go past Queen's apartment *en route* to the Airport." He paused to close the boot of the car, then he added in a joking manner, "I guess she wants to make sure I get on the plane."

"Right you are, Matt!" Khaya was unsure if that was indeed a light-hearted joke or sarcasm, so attempted to respond as diplomatically as possible.

Once settled in the car, Mathew speed dialled Queen. The phone just rang before going to voicemail. He tried again. *She's probably in the shower or something,* he told himself, before leaving a voice message to inform her that he would be by her apartment in about 20-minutes, early traffic permitting.

Khaya drove the car to the collection zone at the front of the prestigious block, but Queen was not standing outside as he expected. Mr Slade seemed to be in a deep conversation with other residents to notice. So, Mathew hurriedly stepped out of the car and up the stairs to ring the external intercom. No answer.

Seriously? Mathew felt a tinge of frustration, *I know things are not going the way we anticipated, but she agreed to at least come to see me off.* Mathew looked at his watch, before remembering the last words he said to her: "to reflect and consider". Perhaps she had done just that and decided it was over between them.

Surprised by the sudden cold shoulder, Mathew returned down the steps muttering to himself, *Well I cannot force her out here!* He got back into the passenger seat.

"Right Khaya, change of plans! It's just the two of us!"

Having left Mathew at the airport departures, Khaya could not stop wondering why Queen would act this way. *She doesn't seem the type of woman to turn a cold shoulder like this, without any explanation.* He decided to go past her apartment on the way back to Mathew's home, which he was housesitting for the next few months.

Khaya double-parked the car and jogged up the steps to try the intercom again. As he stood there waiting for a response, Mr Slade made an appearance through the glass doors.

"Hello Sir, you haven't seen Miss Queen today have you?" Khaya asked curiously.

Mr Slade walked up closer, looking a little troubled. "Oh, I'm so sorry! Miss Queen was taken to the hospital yesterday evening! It's a terrible thing," he said shaking his head.

"Hospital!?" Khaya repeated disbelievingly.

"Indeed! The hospital just around the corner." Mr Slade pointed in the direction of the nearest hospital. "Young Sir, if you are going to see her please send her my wishes for a speedy recovery." Mr Slade asked with sincere sympathy in his voice.

Khaya was still processing this information as he parked in the hospital parking. *So, this was why she hadn't come with Mathew!* He hurried towards the front desk to inquire with the mid-aged woman wearing a badge that read: "My name is Irene. How may I help you?"

"Hello Irene, I'm looking for a young woman who arrived by ambulance last night?" Khaya realised he did not know all the details for Irene to perform a search. "Her name is Queen, but I'm unsure of her surname."

After checking their online system, Irene looked up at Khaya. "I'm afraid I don't have anyone with that name, but there was a young lady brought in last night. She was in and out of consciousness, and she needed sedation for the necessary scans, so we have yet to obtain her details. If you are a family member, I can let you visit."

"Yes! Yes! I am a family member!" Khaya declared, hoping Nurse Irene would not ask why he did not know the surname of his family member.

Irene looked at him sternly. "You are the first family member to visit" She sounded unconvinced. "You need to provide details for the account?" She poked repeatedly to the empty spaces.

As much as Khaya tried to explain that Queen was good for it, the hospital required a credit card and her full details for their records. Unwilling to supply his credit card until he could confirm the patient was indeed Queen.

"Irene, I would be happy to oblige if I could at least see her to confirm?" Khaya asked.

Looking at the clock hanging on the wall behind her, Irene replied sternly. "I'm afraid it is not visiting hours, but I guess I could allow you a few minutes just to clarify."

Khaya quickly navigated his way to the room where Queen lay with her head tilted towards the window. He cleared his throat, as he walked towards her bed, politely acknowledging the older woman lying in the bed opposite with a smile.

"Queen?" he asked quietly so as not to surprise her. Khaya rounded the end of the metal-framed bed, almost gasping when he saw her battered head. "Queen! My God, what happened to you?"

"She can't talk much!" Announced the other woman. "I think it's her ribs, besides, she is pretty drugged up for the head injury. She came in last night."

Khaya wondered why this woman felt like she should be so involved in his visit, but he was thankful for the information.

Queen opened her swollen eyes and looked at Khaya, who had taken her delicate hand in his. He sat down without taking his eyes from her. "Who did this to you?" He questioned her lightly.

"It doesn't matter. It is what it is," Queen said in a breathy broken whisper, "Khaya please go to my place and get me some clothes." She paused momentarily to catch her breath, before speaking in a broken sentence, "blue box ... in my nightstand. Bring that ... Please."

"Of course, Queen I'll be back at visiting hours with everything you need." Khaya stood up and gave her a soft peck on her forehead. Queen smiled inside thinking how sweet that was of him.

"Is there anyone you would like me to call?" He asked. She turned her head gently side to side and closed her eyelids.

"I will see you in a couple of hours. Try to get some rest now," Khaya gave her foot a little squeeze before he left.

Khaya tried to sneak by Irene, who seemed to have the eyes of a golden eagle, she stepped towards him with a clipboard.

"So, is that your family member?" She asked suspiciously.

Khaya responded hurriedly. "Yes, it is," trying to side-step the determined clipboard-wielding receptionist.

"Well, then could we have a credit card number and some patient details please?" Irene insisted.

Reluctantly, Khaya provided his credit card details and promised to get the form fully completed when he returned at visiting hours.

I better call Mathew to let him know, Khaya silently considered the situation as he walked towards the car. He looked at his watch. *Damn, he will be in the air already! I guess I will have to wait for when he checks in with me. Not sure if leaving a voice message with this unpleasant news is the best idea.*

"Here you go young Sir," said the caretaker as he opened the door to Queen's apartment for Khaya. "I got the mess cleaned up. Tragic business this!" He said shaking his head.

"Thank you, I won't be too long. Just here to collect a few things," Khaya said before gently ushering the well-meaning man out the apartment.

Khaya closed the door and turned to survey the living room. "Wow, Queen is doing alright for herself!" He said allowed in astonishment.

Having navigated the passage, Khaya found himself in Queen's boudoir. He felt somewhat awkward being here, never mind selecting clothes for a woman he barely knew. Opening closet door after closet door, he eventually located an outfit he believed would be comfortable. To get a better idea, he laid it out on the bed: black leggings, a white tank top, an olive-green soft cashmere sweater and a pair of bright white sneakers. *Well, that looks comfortable enough, now I just need a bag to put it all in,* he commended himself as he returned to the intimidating corridor of doors.

Khaya hesitated for a moment, before rummaging through her 'intimates' drawer. There lay neatly folded underwear items of every colour and every fabric type. Thumbing through the layers of lace and satin with his fingertips, Khaya felt like this was an invasion of her privacy, but knew he needed to find something less sexy and more comforting considering the circumstances. Next loose-fitting sleepwear, a few grooming products, then her cell phone and charger.

"I know I'm missing something!" Khaya said aloud as he stood attempting to recall Queen's request.

"Aha bedside nightstand, blue box!"

It was a tatty pale-blue box, *What on earth?* Khaya held it firmly in his hands. *Surely not? Better just check it's not something irrelevant or inappropriate.* He lifted the side of the box to take a quick peek. A musty, pungent odour escaped. Inside lay neatly stacked, yet dirty torn banknotes, secured by elastics into bundles.

Crikey there must be close to R25,000 in here! Khaya was puzzled.

Then he noticed two photographs. One, an old snap of a family standing in the sunlight outside of a thatched hut. The other showed a group of young women positioned seductively around a bar, wearing hot-shorts and skimpy vests with: "Mthunzi's Girls" written across the chest.

He took a closer look at the photograph.

"Is that? No surely not … Queen?" Khaya examined the familiar face of the girl leaning against the chrome balustrade in a skimpy black dress, "but it looks just like her?"

Confused and now feeling a twinge of guilt for prying, he closed the box. *I better check the other nightstand in case there is another blue box*, he thought. There was none, so he added this to the leather overnight bag and left the apartment.

CHAPTER NINETEEN

At 03:02pm Khaya entered the clinical smelling ward once more. Queen appeared to be looking much better than earlier. Her chatty roommate was absent, but a new lady was sleeping quietly in the other bed.

"Good Afternoon Beautiful," he beamed as he crossed the shiny floor to Queen's bedside. "How are you feeling this afternoon?" He asked.

Queen smiled and responded in a soft tone, "Hi Khaya. I'm in a lot of pain, but so much better." She paused to catch her breath, "at least my head feels a little clearer ... Thanks."

"Well, here are all the goodies you might need. I didn't know how long you were staying, so I brought extras." He said placing the overnight bag on the hospital chair closest to the bed.

Between intermittent pauses for air, Queen replied. "The Doc says the brain swelling has gone down remarkably well. So, apart from a few bumps and bruises, I have a couple of fractured ribs which can heal at home." She smiled, "I am waiting for them to discharge me now."

Khaya looked surprised and relieved upon hearing the news. "That's great! Now, I don't want you to put up a fuss, but since Matt is gone, I have time to take care of you!"

Khaya was elated at both the prospect of her leaving the hospital, but also that he had the time to make sure she healed. Besides, it would allow him to find out what happened. He took a seat.

Just then the doctor and nurse entered the room holding Irene's precious clipboard.

"Right Miss Mthethwa, you have the OK from me. You should see an improvement within the next two to three weeks, but it will take up to six weeks to fully recover." He smiled down at her, "the nurse will come through in the next few minutes to help you change, then she will wheel you to the 'Accounts Desk'. If you experience any issues give me a call," he said passing her his card.

"Miss Mthethwa, I see you already have a credit card on file to settle the bill, would you like to use that method?" The squeaky sing-songy little voice sang from behind the glass window.

Queen looked confused.

"Oh, that was me!" Khaya said as he placed his hand lightly on her shoulder, "you can leave it and pay me later if you like."

Queen was stunned that Khaya would do that, yet at the same time she was not surprised, he had a generous and kind heart. She looked at the clerk.

"No thank you. I have the cash." She opened the blue box that was on her lap and took out a few bundles of grubby notes which she passed to the clerk. Looking back at Khaya, Queen gave a tired smile and mouthed: "Thanks." She closed the blue box once more.

Khaya patted her should with his hand reassuringly, thinking, *it's bizarre with such wealth, that she chooses to pay in this manner*, then realising it was not his business, he shrugged it off.

Back at the apartment, Khaya helped Queen into her bed. He placed her phone and a glass of water by her bed, then sat next to her. "Queen, I'm going to stay here for a few days, just to help you until you start to heal." He smiled at her, "but don't worry I'll sleep on that comfortable looking couch in your living room."

Realising that she had no one else and feeling as insecure as she did right now Queen was more than willing to have his company.

"I'm not sure if I will be a good patient though, as I have always taken care of myself," she admitted.

Khaya chuckled, "well I'm not so sure I will make a good nurse, so I guess we are even then."

Laying back into the stack of soft pillows, Queen looked up to the ceiling. She took a deep breath.

"I am starving!! I haven't eaten for more than 24-hours and would kill for some Chicken Chow Mein right now!"

"Then let me take a quick dash to the takeaway around the corner and get us some for dinner. Trust me you don't want me cooking for you unless you feel like peanut butter on toast!" Khaya grinned at Queen.

Trying not to laugh she held her hand to her rib cage. "No Khaya don't make me laugh!"

Khaya stood up and put his trendy leather jacket on. "I'll be back in 20 minutes I reckon. Don't go anywhere," he said with a cheeky wink.

Queen heard the front door click closed. She lifted her phone off the nightstand to see four missed calls. Two from Mathew yesterday, one from Kgabu last night and one from Isaac from this morning. She was not in the mood for dealing with any of the men in her life, but Isaac is one she needed to address. *Surely, even Isaac would know that what he did to me was wrong,* she contemplated. Then suddenly an uneasy feeling came over her. *What if Isaac came to the apartment unannounced and found Khaya sleeping here!*

No matter what, she had to contact Isaac, to tell him she needed some time to heal, but did not want to hear his voice. Taking a photo of the hospital bill, Queen sent it to Isaac as proof, along with a message explaining that she was physically unable to speak, and needed bed rest for three weeks. He promptly responded with a message that read:

"Queen, why do you try to make me so angry? I am going away on business for two weeks so I will visit you when I return. I want you too much sometimes that it drives me crazy that I might lose you."

Ugh Please! Typical shifting the blame! Queen felt ill reading that, but at least the coast was clear for the next two weeks. Now she could concentrate on getting better. With that Queen turned off her phone completely.

Just then she heard the familiar click of the front door. Her body tensed, but soon she heard footsteps mixed with the sounds of brown paper packets.

"Hi Honey I'm home!" Khaya's familiar happy voice echoed from the kitchen. In almost no time, he was presenting her with a tray holding her favourite Chinese takeaway, a glass of water and her painkillers. Together they sat eating while Khaya did most, if not all, of the talking. Finally, the sedatives took effect, and Queen drifted off to sleep.

Khaya took the plush knitted throw from the end of Queen's bed and made his way to the lounge.

The next morning, Khaya assisted a bruised and aching Queen to the bathroom. He felt inept being in this position as he removed her cotton pyjamas, trying not to appear as though he was admiring her loveliness even in this damaged state. He sponged her back and shoulders with the warm soapy water, before passing her the sponge to bathe herself, as he left the room.

The sight of this angel's bruised and abused body almost brought tears to his eyes. He just could not comprehend why someone would do that to a woman. This week it was his mission to get to the bottom of this incident. *I need to find out what happened and who is responsible!*

Soon Queen was washed and settled back on her bed, within easy reach of her phone, laptop and TV remote. Khaya placed a glass of water by her bedside.

"As you know, I'm taking care of Matt's place while he is away, so I just have to take a drive there to make sure all is fine. Then I have a few things I need to do, but I will be back with lunch for us." With that, he kissed Queen's forehead and left.

Queen smiled at this sweet gesture he made each time he left. It was innocent and loving, yet so unexpected. He truly was just doing this as part of his kind nature. Queen punched her code into her phone and watched as it sprung to life with a barrage of shrilling notifications. Amongst them was a voicemail from Mathew.

She listened intently.

"Hi Queen, it's Matthew. Khaya got in touch with me last evening and told me that you were in

the hospital! I've been calling to speak to you personally, but your phone is off. This morning, things in the office are pretty hectic as you can imagine. I just ..." He paused to acknowledge someone in his office, *"I'm sorry Queen. I must go. I will try to get hold of you later. Take care of yourself!"*

Lying there with the phone in her hand, Queen realised that this was the first time she had thought of Mathew. She considered her deep feelings for him when in his presence but now felt somewhat distant after their recent discussions and his leaving. *It was stupid of me to think I could start something heartfelt, considering the Isaac-arrangement.* Queen reprimanded herself harshly, *how on earth am I going to get out of this situation.* She held her breath and groaned as she reached for the pale-blue box which was now placed on the nightstand.

Lifting the lid, she looked inside. *Well finally the money came in useful, but there is nothing left for me to break free now. I need to figure out a new escape plan.* She picked up the photographs, remembering these radically different chapters of her life. How her innocence and future potential was dissolved by the reality of what she had endured so far.

She missed those guttural belly laughs with Ayize; Gogo's comfortable hugs; the simplicity of doing the weeks washing at the river edge. Lost in the wonderment of her past life, Queen dozed off as the sedatives carried her to slumber.

"Queen ... Queen," the soft voice of Khaya woke her. She opened her eyes and saw him placing the photographs back into the pale-blue box and placing it on the nightstand. "It's time for lunch," he whispered, as she stirred from a deep sleep.

With a look of pain on her face, Queen sat up slowly arranging the duvet across her legs so that Khaya could place the bed tray for her. "Wow, Khaya! This meal is huge!" Queen's eyes were just as huge as she looked at Khaya, "I can't remember when last I even ate a burger!"

"Good, then you should enjoy it!" Khaya said proudly, as they tucked into their lunch.

"You must know that I have a lot of questions?" Khaya asked between mouthfuls.

Queen nodded. She knew she owed him an explanation.

"Do you think you might be up to answering some of them for me then?" He inquired cautiously.

"Khaya I will try. Just know my life is not an easy story for me to tell, but I owe that much to you." Taking a deep breath, Queen slid her tray with a half-eaten burger to the side.

"It all starts with this blue shoebox." She said reaching to retrieve it once more before passing the pictures one by one to Khaya.

For the next hour, Khaya sat transfixed learning of Queen's sad story. The story of a hopeful, yet struggling young family living in the foothills. She told of a dubious contract robbing the family of the two youngest girls, and how she could never forgive herself for leaving Ayize behind. How the girls were exploited as mere possessions, for the pleasure of men until her escape came in the form of the influential and easily angered Isaac. She explained without providing specific details that there were other, far more considerate men in her life. How she wished for it all to end, so she could finally chase the dream of a drastically different future.

Khaya's emotions ping-ponged from sadness to outright fury, then to empathy. He wished desperately to be her saviour but could not perceive how he could compete with the influential men in her life. He knew none of this was right. Not the contract. Not the holding of these young girls. Not the abuse she suffered. None of it.

"Queen, I have some savings set aside to start my own business one day. I'm not using it so perhaps I can help you? Consider it a loan."

Queen flatly declined. "This is my pit Khaya. I cannot accept your money for my troubles, I need to be the one to break the chain of destruction in my life. Besides, Isaac will not be bought, and he has the connections to find me if I run!"

Queen allowed Khaya to hold her gently in his warm hold. Salty tears streamed down her cheeks. These were the first tears she had cried since leaving Ayize, Zanele and the other girls behind almost two years ago. It felt good to be able to release the pent-up emotions with someone who did not judge her.

After what seemed a short lifetime, Queen lifted her head from Khaya's shoulder and slowly admired his face. They were so close she could feel his breath caressing her cheek, calling her to him. Slowly she put her lips to his and kissed him sweetly. She paused drawing away from him slightly to look into his eyes.

Khaya brushed the tears from her cheeks before he reciprocated with a tender kiss on the lips. He spoke in a soft yet factual tone, "Queen what you have endured in your life, has made you who you are today. You are a true warrior and these scars..." he traced the cut above her eye with his warm fingers, "they show the strength and courage that you have inside to overcome anything. From today we are going to make changes to your life ... together."

That night, just like the last few nights Khaya slept on the couch in the spacious living room, yet sleep escaped him entirely.

Around 09:00am the next morning, Queen's cell phone woke with the familiar ringtone. This time the initials read "K.M."

Ahhh it's Kgabu, Queen thought serenely, *just the man I wanted to talk to.* She answered with a cheery disposition disguising the agony she felt. "Good morning Kgabu."

"Good morning Queen. How are you this fine morning?" He asked calmly.

Taking a deep breath, Queen answered politely, "I'm doing well thanks Kgabu, and I trust you are too?"

"Yes, I'm very well thank you. I just wanted to ask if you were available this evening? I have an impromptu function to go to and would love the honour of your company." Kgabu sounded a little frazzled before continued in a rambling fashion, "I haven't seen you since Cape Town, but I understand it is short notice. So, if you are otherwise preoccupied, I will go solo tonight. We can also rendezvous over dinner another time?"

Queen was aware that she would not make a suitable companion tonight but felt she needed to talk to Kgabu in private. Sooner rather than later.

"Unfortunately, I cannot make it this evening, but I would love to talk to you privately. Do you think you could come to my place tomorrow afternoon?" She responded slowly.

"Afternoon? At your place? Ummm ... I'm sure I can juggle a few meetings around." Kgabu appeared confused, "Sounds serious Queen. How's about two o'clock tomorrow?"

Queen knew Kgabu would be good-natured about the meeting. He was always a very amiable gentleman, even if he was a serial womaniser.

"Perfect! See you tomorrow then," Queen said gratefully.

CHAPTER TWENTY

Respecting Queen's need for privacy, Khaya left before she opened her sleepy eyes. He had taken the time to place a handwritten note on her nightstand that read:

"*Good morning Beautiful. I was awake too early for you, so I've gone to the gym, then to check on Matt's place. I have a great idea! I will explain when I'm back with dinner! XXX PS: you look so adorable when you sleep!*"

As usual, Khaya zest brought a smile to Queens' face. She lay there enjoying the safe indulgence of her warm duvet cocoon, appreciating how perfect it was to wake with a sweet note such as this. On further reflection, it dawned on her how empty her life was, living alone amongst her 'expensive things'.

Staring at the stark white ceiling above, she uttered with a discontented tone, "MY things?" In truth, apart from the gifts bestowed on her, Queen owned little of anything. She shut her heavy eyes. "Well, this sham of a life is about morph into something far more authentic!" She whispered aloud.

It was now close to 02:00pm on Thursday. Mr Slade just notified Queen that her visitor was on his way up.

Seated on the broad arm of the couch, Queen waited tentatively for Kgabu to arrive. She attempted to disguise the numerous bruises as best she could, but the stitches above her eye were impossible to hide, as was the pain she endured with every movement. Deep in thought, she rehearsed a myriad of solutions in her mind.

Just then an assertive knock at the door broke the silence.

Through the peephole, Queen saw the unmistakable warrior-like physique standing in the corridor. She opened the door with a polite smile and greeted Kgabu.

Stepping inside the immaculate apartment, Kgabu's eyes instinctively saw through the makeup and pretence.

"Queen! What the hell happened to you?" He asked with a concerned frown on his face, and a tinge of anger in his voice.

Shuffling slowly, while supporting her side, Queen ushered Kgabu towards the living room. "Please make yourself comfortable. I have something important to discuss with you," she articulated in a fragmented sentence.

"Thank you for coming to see me. Firstly, I would like to avoid getting into the details of why I look this way." She said matter-of-factly.

"OK then ..." Kgabu sounded perplexed.

"As you are aware from our last meaningful conversation, I want to exit this lifestyle." Queen offered Kgabu a tall glass of iced tea, before carefully sitting.

"Yes, you mentioned so in Cape Town." Kgabu agreed.

"Well, you mentioned that I could come to you if I needed anything." Queen proceeded guardedly, "So I have a plan if you could hear me out?"

Placing the iced tea on the coffee table, Kgabu stood to remove his tailor-made navy-blue jacket and laid it neatly on the back of the seat next to him.

"Sure Queen, I'm all yours ... At least for the next hour or so. Tell me what you need." He confidently sat down once again, studying her broken appearance as she spoke.

Queen always admired the profound respect Kgabu, this great business mogul, had provided her: the insignificant girl from the foothills of KwaZulu-Natal.

She began to explain her plan, between short pauses to breathe. "With your approval, I would like to sell the gifts which you have so generously provided to me. That would include that colourful masterpiece hanging in the entranceway. As much as I would hate to part with it, I know it's worth."

She watched him listening carefully. "With the proceeds, I want to fund going to college to finish school, and possibly a deposit for a small second-hand car. I will get a job too, but I wonder if you could assist me by way of an interest-bearing loan? That would allow me to rent a small apartment and provide me with stability to get on my feet?" She held her breath as she hesitantly waited for his response.

The afternoon sun was just making its way into the lounge area by this time, throwing golden warmth against the couch like a glowing halo. Queen thought how apt it appeared, for at this given moment she was asking Kgabu to be her guardian angel.

After a short contemplative silence, Kgabu spoke softly. "My beautiful Queen. If I ever had a daughter, I would hope that she would have been half the woman you are! As I have said before, you are worth so much more than this life, but ..." He faltered, "but it is not to say that I have not enjoyed our unfathomable friendship, for that is what it is."

He sat forward on the couch with his elbows on his knees and his one hand cradling his chin, thinking.

Then looking at her, he continued in a more business-like tone. "Firstly, feel free to sell any of the gifts I have given to you. They are yours to do with as you like. As for accommodation? I have numerous businesses, and some of those businesses own corporate suites that stand empty for most of the year. So, I would gladly arrange one of the lesser-used suites to be made available to you."

Kgabu looked about the fabulous apartment he now sat, "It will not be as glamorous as what you are used to, but to compensate I'm thinking no rental for the first six months, then a reduced rent for the following six months. That should afford you ample time."

Queen opened her mouth to speak, but before she could, Kgabu raised his gentle hand to stop her talking.

"Wait, Queen! You are a bright woman so once you have your matric certificate, we can see if any of the university bursaries my companies offer, will fit within your desired career path. At least you will know there is employment waiting for you after you graduate, and you could intern during the vacations if you wish." Queen consistently nodded as she listened to Kgabu unveil his well-considered solution, with utter sincerity.

By this time Queen was doing a lot of what she had been doing these past few days: crying.

"Kgabu, I don't know how to begin to thank you for your continued generosity. I will not let you down. Thank you!" She hoped he recognised her genuine appreciation in every word she spoke. The tears of gratitude began to fall from the wells in her eyes.

"My dear, when you are ready, give me a call and I will put you in touch with our rental agent, no strings attached," Kgabu said assertively, as he stood to put his jacket back on. "I'm thankful that we can see beyond what we have had up until now and welcome in a new level of relationship. So, no more tears, it is a new beginning. Perhaps it is a new chapter for both of us Queen."

Straining to stand up from the couch, Queen emitted a breathy groan, she stepped towards Kgabu to give him a one-armed hug. "Thank you from the bottom of my heart Kgabu. Thank you for also respecting my privacy of this predicament."

With that Kgabu took one last look at the vibrant modern painting in the entrance hall as he put his jacket back on and with a raising of his hand, he left her apartment.

After enjoying Khaya's almost successful attempt at a chicken and broccoli pasta bake, Queen made herself comfortable in the lounge to hear of Khaya's 'great idea'. From his black and grey canvas backpack, he removed an ominous-looking packet and placed it on the couch next to him.

"Well, today I went to some interesting places and spoke to a few experts." He announced quite confidently. "Firstly, I got you one of these!" He said holding up a box containing a stun gun and a pepper spray. "Please don't laugh, but I would honestly feel better knowing you have these in case anyone tries to hurt you again!"

Queen was shocked that the notion of defending herself from Isaac's attacks, had not even entered her mind. Had she become so conditioned by the lifestyle, that she accepted the abuse as a means to her survival?

"No laughing from me! Thanks, so much Khaya!" She said taking the box from him to inspect.

"and then ... I got you one of these!" He said excitedly, ensuring to keep it hidden from view, "But before I show you, promise me you won't get mad!"

After assuring Khaya that she would not be angry at his attempt to keep her from harm, he proudly produced a covert spy camera.

"Just in case Queen! At least we will have some proof if he tries to hurt you again. I also signed up for the information recorded to be kept on 'the cloud'. So, there is no way he can get his hands on it even if he tried."

Speechless at first, Queen just looked at Khaya and then at the box he was holding. "I don't know what to say Khaya! If only you knew how much this means to me that you would worry about my safety!" Queen shook her head slowly disbelieving how caring this gesture was.

By this time, Khaya was grinning broadly and looking like the cat that finally got the cream. "Well, that's all the gift-giving for now, but I have even more to tell you!" He said removing the camera from the packaging and laying out the bit and pieces on the table.

"Gosh, you have been busy today. I'm intrigued!" Queen sat listening to Khaya.

"So, as you know, I am studying at university," he began. "Well, I am in my final year as a law student and have interned at a legal practice a few times. I got in touch with one of the partners to ask for some advice."

Queen felt a queasiness creeping up on her.

"Don't panic I didn't mention any names or places." Khaya looked quite intense now.

"Anyway, Frank reckons that we must get the police involved regards to the operations at Mthunzi's Tavern. It is kidnapping Queen! You must get a restraining order against Isaac. It's not too late to report the..." Khaya was still talking when Queen interrupted him.

"It's impossible! Isaac protects Mthunzi's and as for a docket at the police station? That will just be 'conveniently' lost! Such things will infuriate Isaac beyond anger! No way!" Queen was both stunned and disappointed at Khaya's suggestion.

Khaya waited for Queen to finish reacting, before continuing excitedly. "I understand ... but let me finish first!"

Queen bit her lip and shook her head slowly.

Khaya took a sip of water, before he continued, "So this is Frank's 'unofficial' recommendation. I am going to visit this "Mr Mthunzi" at his place of business. I will explain that there is a law firm in Pretoria with the detailed specifics of his operations, and proof of collusion with a politician. The law firm will release these details to the press and the Priority Crime Unit if Ayize is not released to me immediately."

Queen watched and listened.

"Trust me, Queen! Releasing one girl is not worth the disruption Mthunzi will experience through press and investigations. These allegations are severe, so 'the rats will leave the sinking ship'. Isaac will distance himself rather rapidly from Mthunzi. Once we have Ayize safely away, we can look at putting a halt to the entire operation through other means!"

Still biting her lip Queen considered the suggestion momentarily. She looked up at Khaya studying his gaze.

"Okay! Let's do it! He will know it's me, but I have nothing to lose. Just my sister to gain!"

CHAPTER TWENTY-ONE

It's a bright new day filled with all new possibilities, Queen reassured herself as she opened the bedroom curtains to admire the sunrise. She gently stretched her body, realising how much of a difference a week had already made. The cuts and bruises were fading, but her side stilled ached terribly.

Looking at her appearance in the bathroom mirror, it appeared that after healing, a scar would likely remain just above her eye. Queen felt the hardened ridge with her fingertips, reminding herself: *every brave warrior wears at least one scar of their victory. So, wear it proudly!*

Khaya had just left for Durban by car, promising to call her as soon as there was something to report.

Queen put her fluffy gown on and sauntered through to the kitchen to make some coffee. While the kettle boiled, she folded the knitted throw which Khaya left lying haphazardly on the couch. As she turned towards the kitchen her eyes were instinctively drawn to the new addition on her bookshelf, the covert camera neatly disguised. If she had not helped place it there, she would never have even noticed it. It was hard to comprehend how the small gadget gave her some feeling of security.

It was around 10:00am when Queen's cell phone lit up with an unrecognisable international number. She answered apprehensively.

"Hi, Queen! Can you hear me?" Mathew sounded like he was calling her from the bottom of a well.

Queen pressed the cell phone closer to her ear, "Yes! Hi, Mathew! I can hear you! How are things going?" Trying to ignore the intermittent pain she experienced with the simple task of talking.

"Good! Sorry, it has taken me so long to get back to you! Especially considering the situation down there. Things up here are not appearing as seamless as I planned." Mathew rambled on in a rushed manner, "Ugh, it looks like three months was way too optimistic. On reflection, I will need to personally oversee this set up for at least the first year."

Queen could hear a frazzled tone in Mathew's voice she had not heard before. "But enough about me, how are you doing? What is going on there?" He enquired with concern.

It was that exact moment when Queen realised, she no longer felt the emotional connection with Mathew. Quickly considering whether to tell him of her plans, she decided to avoid the topic altogether.

Instead, she replied tactfully. "Oh, I'm healing well actually! It's a stupid thing! I wasn't paying attention where I was going and took a tumble down the building steps. Turns out that apart from the embarrassment suffered from sprawling on the pavement, I have a fractured rib and an array of bruises. It looks much worse than it is." Queen hoped Mathew would believe her, and that Khaya had not relayed too many specifics of the incident.

"Well, that's good that you are on the mend. I was concerned as Khaya was panicky when I spoke with him, but he said didn't know the details of what transpired!" Mathew was relieved that Queen was healing, and soon probed Queen for some reassurance, "Well probably best I'm away then, or else I would be by your bedside making a nuisance of myself?"

Queen was quiet.

Sensing an air of apprehension, Mathew reacted, "Queen?" and before she could reply, he asked guardedly, "Things aren't going to work between us, are they?"

Queen sighed deeply. "Mathew, I wish things were different. I truly do," she answered him tenderly, "but I cannot change my past. As someone recently said to me, the history of my life has made me who I am today."

Queen struggled but knew she needed to make the break. "I think your business has taken you away for a reason. I am not sure if I can wait a year to start something that just 'might be'." She took a shallow breath before continuing, "Mathew, I think for the time being we should see it for what it is: a close friendship."

This time it was Mathew's turn to be quiet. He responded a little broken. "As usual you are right Queen. Besides, I have my hands full here with little time for distraction, which wouldn't be fair to you. So, friends, it is. We will just have to wait and see what the future brings."

Around midday, Khaya sent a message that he had arrived at the Tavern parking lot. Since then, Queen consistently checked her phone to make sure she did not miss a call from him. By 03:10pm the suspense was killing her. It crossed her mind that something may have happened to Khaya, after all, these people were criminals.

If I haven't heard from him by 03:30pm, I am going to phone him! Fortunately, Queen did not need to wait much longer.

"Queen I have her!" Were the first words from his mouth.

Queen's heart stopped. "Oh Khaya, thank God! Please let me speak to her!"

Khaya responded quite firmly, "I don't think that is a good idea right now Queen. She is not in a good way! In fact, I'm taking her directly to a nearby rehabilitation centre. She will be okay Queen. She just needs some professional care and time to heal herself."

Queen's heart was beating out of her chest, and her hands were trembling. "I can't believe he just let her go!" Queen uttered in disbelief.

Khaya pondered whether to tell her and then did, "Queen, I'm sorry to say that Mthunzi referred to her as 'a dead weight now, just like her mother'. As I expected he was glad for me to take her and save him the problem of dealing with her."

Queen felt helpless being so far away but knew that Khaya had an honest heart, and level-headedness to handle this situation.

"I know I say this a lot but thank you Khaya!" she said wanting to add the words "I love you," but held them back. Tears began to form in her eyes for not saying how she felt, but her fears would not compel her to utter them.

Having now seen the operations at Mthunzi's first-hand, Khaya now understood how Queen had lost her way.

"No worries, this is all going to work out in the end. Just hang in there! I must go Queen, as I need to find this Rehab Centre. I'll be driving back up tomorrow. I just want to stop in and see a good friend of mine. I'll speak to you later." He said raising his voice above the sounds of the afternoon traffic.

Queen responded promptly, "Speak soon! Please drive carefully!"

Unable to sleep, Queen lay awake since 04:00am. Carefully sipping her second steamy mug of coffee, she wondered how her sister was doing this morning. Her thoughts then wandered to Khaya as she considered how grateful she was to have him in her life at this given moment. How she had almost said: "I love you."

Around 9:30am, Queen checked her emails. There were a few emails from Candice, Kgabu's corporate letting agent. Unable to view the properties in her current state, Queen had asked Candice to kindly email her the details of the available units. As Kgabu explained, the premium units were used for the letting portfolio, but this did not deter Queen at all. She felt grateful for the offer, believing that no one should start their life at the top anyway. She was happy to watch her life finally unfold the way it should have five years ago. *Five years already! It seems like a lifetime ago*, she whispered.

After some deliberation, Queen finally selected the small, second-floor one-bedroom flat in Randburg. Not only was this flat close to the college to which she had applied, but the future rental would not break the bank either. Having decided, Queen sat back thinking how her life was changing so rapidly, and yet the biggest obstacle of all had not been dealt with. Isaac was due to return the following week, so Queen still had time to prepare.

For the rest of the day, Queen moved from room to room selecting items she wished to sell to help fund her new life and which she would leave behind. The ever-present problem of Isaac was never far from her mind, although having Khaya by her side made coping far more manageable.

Standing in the entrance hall admiring the abstract masterpiece hanging on the wall, Queen was transfixed by the beauty of the broad strokes when the entrance door swung open behind her. She jumped from fright before she recognised Khaya's happy face. Instantly her heart skipped a beat.

"I missed you!" She said enthusiastically. Before Khaya could even put his backpack down, Queen was holding him as tight and close as her pain would allow.

Khaya wrapped his arms around her, and whispered into her neck, "Oh girl, I've missed you madly! But to be honest, I am completely exhausted."

"I bet you are! It's been a hectic few days. Why don't you take a shower then we can talk," Queen suggested.

"I just wanted to check in with you first to let you know everything. Then I need to go over to Matt's place." Khaya put his backpack down and removed his leather jacket. "Matt messaged me earlier, saying that he needed to video chat with me tonight. So, it's probably best I do that from his place."

"Oh! Alright then." Queen attempted not to sound disappointed, as she just wished to cuddle up to Khaya tonight.

Khaya began offering an update on his trip to Durban.

"So, Ayize is going to be okay. The counsellor said we could fetch her in 12-weeks or so, which is great news."

"Yes! It's the best choice considering her condition." She took Khaya's hand and sat on one of the kitchen stools facing him.

He smiled at her, before continuing, "Then as you know, I visited with my mate, 'T-Bar'. He is an over-zealous investigative journalist friend. I thought he would be interested in doing some groundwork on our situation, possibly an exposé. He is most eager, but reckons it will take a couple of months for him and his team to gather all the data."

Queen squeezed his hand, "To be honest, I'm a little afraid Khaya."

"Don't be, they will be discreet about it and will show it as being findings from their investigations." Squeezing her hand back, Khaya responded light-heartedly "Besides, you got me to protect you now, and I'm not going anywhere. Sorry pretty lady, but you're stuck with me!" Khaya stood up, embracing Queen once more.

He whispered softly into her ear, "I love you, Queen. From the moment I saw you, I knew I loved you."

As much as she wanted to shout out: "I love you to Khaya!", Queen could not bring herself to utter those simple words. She hung to him silently, listening to the rhythmic thumping of his healthy heart.

The apartment once again appeared desolate without Khaya. Queen fastened the chain of the door behind him. Using the door chain was something she recently began to do when not up and about the apartment. She turned off the lights and left the living room to soak away her worries in a candlelit bubble bath.

CHAPTER TWENTY-TWO

Lately, Queen rose earlier than usual, almost unable to relax in bed. Watching the city come to life whilst wrapped in a warm towelling gown, appeared far more appealing. Not sure when Khaya would return, she unlatched the chain of the front door, then flicked the switch which brought the kettle to life. She sauntered through the living room to open the balcony terrace doors. She took as deep a breath as she could feeling the crispness of the morning air.

She looked down at the early morning runners. *Now that I won't have a gym membership anymore, perhaps I'll be like those crazy ants down there and take up running.* She gave a little chuckle at the ludicrous idea of her feet religiously pounding the pavement.

Queen heard the familiar click of the kettle. She adjusted the belt of her plush towelling gown and turned to make her coffee. Standing in the middle of her living room was the menacing figure of Isaac. She stopped, stunned by his early return. Queen was not sure what to do, but she knew she certainly did not want to be on the terrace!

Without taking her eyes off him, Queen moved slowly into the living room, pulling the sliding door closed behind her.

"Hello Isaac," she said unemotionally.

"Oh! I see you can talk now!" He responded aggressively. "Good, then you can provide me with some answers!"

Queen was instinctively aware of the covert camera and reminded herself that she was to avoid leaving this room at all costs. The pepper spray was in her handbag, and the stun gun was next to her bed, both too far away to be of any use. For now, the glass coffee table was all that separated them.

"Last night I had a call from your old boss in Durban!" Isaac emitted the words viciously as he stepped towards her. "Care to explain?"

Queen stood still. Noticing him making his way around the table, she moved to keep the table between them. "I don't know what you are talking about, Isaac." She uttered defiantly to disguise her terror.

"Lying bitch!" He spewed. "Then why would threats to expose my dealings with Mthunzi, revolve around the release of YOUR sister!" He roared with rage.

Having no comeback, Queen looked down like a cornered puppy as she considered making a break to the bedroom to get the stun gun. With that, Isaac forcefully lifted the glass table and flipped it out the way as he charged at her. Amidst the chaotic splintering of glass, she attempted to slip past him. Isaac grabbed her from behind and threw her towards the bookshelf. Filled with adrenalin, Queen spun around, only to have Isaac pin her against the bookshelf. With his hands clutching either side of her head, he questioned her with a look of violence in his dark eyes.

"Who are you working with Queen? Who?" He demanded. Isaac began shaking her fiercely by the throat, shouting. "Tell me Queen or I'm going to kill you!" So brutal was the shaking that Queen could feel the excruciating pain rising as her healing bones began to crack. He threw her against the frame of the upturned coffee table. She gasped for her breath.

Isaac seized Queen by the hair, lifting her to her feet once more. Her knees bloodied by shards of glass. With his enraged face right up close to hers, he spat threateningly. "I warned you last time, not to make me angry! Why do you do this to me, knowing I will destroy you!?"

He lifted his hand to hit her, this time Queen turned her body raising her arm in defence. She looked directly into his face, "C'mon hit me again Isaac! Kill me! I dare you!" she shouted bravely.

Isaac stopped, with his fist raised and looked at her quizzically, "What are you up to?"

She pointed towards the bookshelf. Isaac turned instinctively to look. Noticing the small shiny lens of the concealed camera. He glared at Queen as she started to laugh, "You can do nothing

Isaac Mopantokobogo! Nothing! It's all on 'the cloud'!"

As the implications began to sink into his head, Isaac began to lower his fist but did not loosen his tight grip on her arm.

"Nothing? Remember, I own you, Queen!" He growled at her, "You have until midday to get out of this apartment. Go live on the streets as you deserve! No one will want you! You are soiled goods!"

With that, Isaac stormed out of the apartment he had provided to Queen for the duration of their arrangement.

A wounded yet defiant Queen had stood her ground against the great beast! She had finally beaten him at his own game.

CHAPTER TWENTY-THREE

It was exactly three months and three days later when Queen found herself leaning impatiently against Khaya's car in the car park of the Durban rehab centre. The midday sun blazed down warming her back. Her eyes remained fixed on the front door.

Queen's heart was thumping like crazy, growing more intense with every second. *Today is a new beginning for Ayize! A new beginning for us!* It was now four years since she had seen her sister.

Khaya took Queen's hand in his and held it tightly. He realised that she was anxious to see her sister after all these years. Then the door opened. Queen slowly released her tight grip of Khaya's hand and stepped towards the building entrance. Ayize stood in the arch of the doorway looking like the little-lost farm girl of 18 again.

Queen ran from the car, up the steps to Ayize. She hugged her with all her heart.

"I've missed you, my sister!" Queen cried. For the first time in a long time, Queen felt Ayize's arms wrapped around her.

"I've missed you to my sister."

Khaya watched the two sisters hug each other as if their actual lives depended on it. Queen sobbed, "I'm so sorry I left you Ayize! I'm so sorry."

"What matters now is we are together again Mbali!" Ayize responded.

Khaya wondered silently, *Mbali? This is the first time I have heard this name.*

Soon, the two Mthethwa girls were bundled safely together on the back seat of Khaya's car. Holding each other's hands tightly, they spoke quietly with expressions of disbelief. Khaya navigated the vehicle with the aid of a GPS towards Gogo Isisa's humble home hidden amongst the rolling green foothills of KwaZulu-Natal.

The metallic blue of Khaya's car sparkled in the midday sun. It crossed the bridge over the gushing river and ambled up the steep dirt road to the thatched mud hut. The two young women sat hand in hand, quietly peering out the window. Some happy chickens ran freely collecting the bugs from the wildflowers which edged the impeccably swept sandy ground of the platform around the humble dwelling.

A sad and bent-over old lady stood outside with a walking stick. Around her hips, a well-worn fleece blanket was wrapped snuggly. Her head was swathed in a fraying *shweshwe* fabric, with just a glimpse of curly grey hair peeping out from beneath. The old lady had curiously watched the blue car winding its way up from the bottom of the dirt road.

She remembered the sad day when a stranger in a blue car had turned her life upside down.

The car gentled rolled to a stop. Khaya got out of the car, acknowledging her with a nod and a bright smile. She watched him intently, as he opened the back door and let out his precious cargo. Gogo's eyes grew big and teary as she began to wail loudly. The two young ladies ran to Gogo, to hug and kiss her on her tear-stained wrinkled cheeks.

It was then that another familiar face appeared from the pathway leading from behind Gogo's home. It was Mandla. He had grown into a good-looking young man. He was now the age that Mbali was when she had left her family on that fateful day.

"Where is Mama?" Ayize asked.

Gogo looked at the two beautiful faces she held in her frail hands and answered softly, "I'm sorry my children. The heavens took your mother, not even five days after you left."

Holding both their hands for stability, Gogo led her granddaughters to the rock at the edge of the garden. The giant rock where the family once sat listening to Nandi sharing her imaginative stories. The view of the river and the sunset was always best from this viewpoint. The unassuming resting site of heaped boulders, decorated lovingly with vibrant yellow wildflowers, was pure and genuine to the spirit of Nandi.

Gogo spoke again, squeezing their hands tightly, "She is at peace now my children. Don't be sad, because she is smiling now that you are both home again."

It was a little later while enjoying the meagre meal that Gogo had lovingly prepared that Mbali learnt that her two older sisters were happy with their simple lives. They still worked at the retreat hotel, and both had married decent hardworking men. Mandla was proving to be proficient at his schooling and was working with a local farmer during the holidays to learn the skills of rearing ducks and chickens.

Although he was just 16, Mandla dreamed to one day have his own farm. He decided to go to agricultural college after school, and a generous farmer agreed to sponsor him in exchange for him feeding his livestock on weekends.

Mbali smiled at Mandla. "I'm so proud of you my brother! I am also back at school now, but it seems you have caught up with me!" She said poking him jokingly.

Khaya was quietly admiring the deep love this little family had for each other. How they accepted and encouraged the dreams and ambitions each held far beyond their simple life. He now understood why Queen, whom he learnt was born as Mbali, was so caring and thoughtful, but also the most courageous and resilient woman he knew.

Although she was beautiful on the outside, it was her inner beauty he truly fell in love with.

After what seemed too little time, the sun was about to set, and it was time to leave. Mbali reached into her handbag to retrieve an envelope which she passed to Mandla.

"Mandla, as the man of the house this is for you to use to take care of Gogo and Ayize. Spend it wisely."

Then hugging them all goodbye, Mbali promised to return during the holidays once she completed her schooling. She hugged Ayize tighter than ever before.

"My sister, you take care now. You must continue to get better so you can also enjoy your second chance! I will see you soon."

Khaya booked a night at the hotel where the sisters worked, to allow Queen to visit with them before they left in the morning.

It was during the trip back to Johannesburg that Khaya broached the topic of the visit.

"Queen, I noticed that your family call you 'Mbali' and was wondering if you wanted to tell me about that?"

Queen was quiet at first, then answered him hesitantly. "Well Khaya, Mbali was my given name, but my adult life I have used Queen. It would feel strange to be called anything else now."

"I see." He answered, "But wouldn't you rather close that chapter entirely now? Start fresh?"

Queen sighed as she looked at the green fields passing swiftly by the windows, and replied gently, "Perhaps."

It was Khaya who spoke again. "Your family has such love. I only wish my family had such feeling."

"I'm sure your parents love you just as much Khaya," she responded. "Some people just don't show it so openly as others."

Khaya thought about it briefly before speaking, "Maybe you are right, but sometimes it feels like it is more about keeping up with the neighbours. I think my brother is that way too."

After a few silent minutes, Khaya spoke again, more assertively. "Queen, I would like you to meet my family. I think it is time. We have been seeing each other 'officially' for almost two months, and now I've met your family."

Queen looked over and smiled.

"I'd like that Khaya. Very much!" Lifting his hand to her mouth she brushed it gently with her lips, whispering ever so quietly: "I Love you."

He smiled, knowing that his patience was paying off, little by little. Queen was blossoming into her true self. He quietly mulled over the future that lay ahead for them. *One day I would be proud to make her my wife. That much I know for sure!* Khaya's heart felt more alive than ever.

CHAPTER TWENTY-FOUR

The shady tree-lined avenue cut through rows of towering mansions locked behind eight-foot walls. Queen was nervous. She had never met the family of a boyfriend. In fact, she had never actually had a boyfriend.

The car slowed and turned, stopping behind an ornately designed wrought iron gate. A double-storey Tuscan inspired home was discreetly tucked away at the end of a long cobble-stoned driveway. Queen was aware of the monotonous purring of the car engine whilst waiting for the automatic gate to tick open.

"Well, we are here!" Khaya said proudly. The car gradually began winding way up the drive. Queen nervously pressed the creases from her dress with the clammy palms of her hands. Moving ever closer to the mansion, Queen's expression changed to one of surprise.

This is like something out of an upmarket lifestyle magazine. I cannot believe Khaya comes from such wealth. Queen felt her anxiety level rise even more.

"This is the place I grew up in." Khaya attempted to break the silence. He looked over to Queen and noticed her hands fidgeting anxiously.

"No need to be nervous, Babe. It's just my family, not a job interview!" He chortled.

The car stopped. Standing at the door was a regal looking lady. She was tall, slim and exceptionally well dressed in bright designer-wear. Next to her stood a teenage boy, dressed in trendy street style attire, with what seemed to be expensive DJ headphones looped around his neck.

"Everyone, this is my queen," Khaya said proudly making his way up the entrance steps, "and this is my beautiful mother, Faith, and my brat of a younger brother, Siyanda," Khaya said.

Queen greeted them politely with a brief hug before Faith welcomed them into the elegant home. Crossing the stone-tiled foyer, they made their way through to the formal lounge complete with a fireplace and a 180-degree view of the perfectly manicured garden. Queen sat on the comfortable couch, feeling a little like a fish out of water. To ease her anxiety, Khaya sat next to her with his hand on her knee.

"Khaya tells me you are registering for university for next year?" Faith asked.

Trying not to feel inadequate, Queen responded. "Yes, that's right! I am enrolling to study psychology. In the meantime, I work at a family-run Italian restaurant. They are trying to teach me Italian!" She smiled broadly realising she was rambling in her attempt to avert the part where she was only now finishing her final school year.

"Psychology?" Faith replied, "That's interesting! I was majoring in psychology when I met Khaya's father. Unfortunately, I never actually got to utilise my degree though. Any idea what you plan to do after that?"

Queen smiled. "Indeed, I do! I would like to start a foundation that allows me to visit rural schools, to offer guidance to young girls. I hope to prepare them with social skills, as well as the opportunity to meet mentors who can assist in obtaining bursaries or internships. I just want to prevent young girls from falling through the cracks in society."

Faith listened attentively. "That is admirable. It's an emotionally demanding area, but if you require any assistance, I would be more than happy to get involved." She smiled sincerely. "After all, I am well connected to people with deep pockets."

Queen wondered if Khaya had inherited his beautiful smile from his mother or his father.

Khaya broke the ensuing silence. "Mom? Where's Dad?" Khaya asked quizzically.

"I think he is doing what he does best. Always in the office that one!" She responded with raised eyebrows and a shake of the head, then added with more cheer, "Although I must be honest, I don't know what has come over him lately. He has been quite a devoted husband these days. Turned over a new leaf that one!"

Khaya stood up. "I'm just going to get us something to drink. I'll be back in a moment." He winked at Queen before leaving the room.

A few minutes passed before Queen heard footsteps walking through the corridor behind her.

"Ah, talk of the devil, here he is!" Faith smiled fondly as a strong shadow neared the room.

A moment prematurely, Queen stood up from the couch and turned to face the arched doorway, just as a tall and dignified gentleman entered.

Their eyes met with unique familiarity. Queen being quick to react to potentially awkward situations, attempted to disguise her disbelief. She smiled brightly as she leant forward holding out her delicate hand.

"It's an honour to meet you, Mr Mokae, I'm Mbali Mthethwa!"

With their eyes transfixed on each another, each shared an unspoken moment of gratitude and understanding. Mr Mokae extended his warm hand to welcome Mbali to his home, and his family.

"Please Mbali," he smiled, "call me Kgabu."

-The End-

If you enjoyed the tale of Mbali, please be so kind as to leave a quick review (link below). I would love to hear from you.

Thank you! Ngiyabonga! (Zulu)

https://www.amazon.com/review/create-review/edit?ie=UTF8&channel=glance-detail&asin=B076CMFLXM

Facebook: EsjayCMoore

Other Books
The Making of Mya

www.ingramcontent.com/pod-product-compliance
Lightning Source LLC
Chambersburg PA
CBHW011456170626
46814CB00009B/3070